Nowhere

To

RUN

Nowhere To RUN

STOLEN Series Book 2

Lisa Murphy

Disclaimer & Copyright

This is a work of fiction. Names, characters, businesses, places, events and incidents are either products of the author's imaginations, or used in a fictitious manner. Any resemblance to actual people, living or dead, or actual events, is purely coincidental.

Copyright © 2020 Lisa Murphy

Cover illustration, design, and photography by Lisa Murphy. Front cover model, Dakota Teague. Back cover model Brittne Briscoe. All rights reserved.

Dedication

God: Thank you.

My Aunts, Wilena Nice and Willa Kowal: Thank you for taking the time to listen and all your support. I love you both.

Mark, Brent, Shanna, Zoey, Jase, Eli, and Vance: I love you ALL as far as the east is from the west.

Donna Murphy: Thank you for taking so much time to help. You went far beyond the extra mile. I appreciate it so much! I love you too!

Dakota and Brittne: Thank you both, for being such good sports and wonderful models.

Chapter 1

Missouri 1890

    The wagon jolted to a hard stop, causing dust to flood inside the stagecoach. Abby quickly covered her nose to block the fog of dust that surrounded her. Using her free hand, she swiftly waved a small accordion fan, to push the filthy air away.
    As the dusty haze slowly began to settle, things again became visible. Being the only passenger on the Pioneer Line Stagecoach, Abby Gibbs was ready to see people, anyone after weeks of being cooped up during her trip. She eagerly peered out the open window.
    At long last she had arrived at her new home, Cedar Creek, Missouri. She felt in her heart,

at first glance, that this would be a pleasant place to live. Abby took note of every detail of her new surroundings. The storefronts were well maintained with their boardwalks neatly swept.

Wood benches sat snuggly against several of the buildings. Old whiskey barrels, cut in half, lined the boardwalks. Each barrel was filled with beautiful blooming flowers of various colors.

Abby looked toward the mill. She watched as the water wheel turned in a circle, over and over, causing the water to make a rippling sound. Abby thought it quite soothing. As her eyes roamed the town her excitement grew.

Glancing toward the opposite end of town Abby noticed a row of four small houses on each side of the road. Each one had a wooden flower box hanging under the front window. Like the barrels, each box was filled with lovely flowers. Abby loved flowers and thought they made everything brighter.

White picket fences surrounded the little cottages. Green ivy vines and honeysuckle spread across the fencing. Taking a deep breath, she could smell its sweet aroma.

As her eyes roamed around, she spotted a pink rose bush growing beside one of the fence gates. Abby thought how wonderful it would be to enjoy the fresh scent of roses each time you passed through the gate.

One of the houses had a door that was painted blue. She had never seen a door painted that color before, but she liked it. Her attention was drawn toward giggles and laughter nearby. Two children were playing happily together. Such a joyful sound, she thought as she listened. Such a peaceful place, she smiled to herself.

An occasional bird chirped a cheerful melody. Abby studied the row of adorable little cottages for a few minutes. She felt it would be a dream come true to live in one of them, on the edge of this utterly charming town.

Glancing around she noticed two older gentlemen seated on a bench near the stables. She watched as they chatted with each other, smiling occasionally. Abby imagined that each man was telling tall tales to each other as a way to pass the time.

People walked past the coach, going about their daily life. Being new to Cedar Creek, Abby took it all in. A young mother and her son hurried past her window toward the opposite end of town, away from the row of charming homes. The mother held on to her son's hand as they rushed away. Abruptly stopping, the young mother leaned down toward the little boy and spoke a few words that Abby couldn't hear. The son nodded his head and they began to walk on again.

Abby wondered what it would be like to be a mother? Saddened by this thought, she would never know. The doctor had said that she could never bare children. Wesley Roberts face, his wrath and violent acts, stabbed her heart. Although free from the past, it still found ways to haunt her.

She watched as the child and his mother neared the edge of town. They turned onto a worn narrow trail that led up a small hillside. Abby's eyes followed the path, to see where it led.

How had she missed that, she wondered? The path went straight to a quaint little church, nestled under several large oak trees. This was an important discovery. Not only was this where she would be the new school teacher, it was also going to be her home for the next year.

In the letter that Pastor Johnson had sent to her, he had explained that the entire town was excited to have a teacher. So happy in fact, that many of the families joined together donating building supplies, labor, and food for a barn raising day. Actually, in this case, they called it a teacher's quarters day. A new room was added to the side of the church, so Abby would have a place to stay when she arrived.

She had mixed feelings about living at the church. On one hand, it would be nice not to have to walk to school in bad weather. She hated walking in snow, rain and thunderstorms, especially when there was lightning.

Not having to travel in the dark was a definite plus in her eyes. She wasn't scared of it, but at times it was difficult to see the road. Wild animals prowled around in the cover of darkness. She preferred to see where she was going and who or what was around her. Being a bear's morning snack wasn't on her list of things to do.

Her mind pondered a few of the drawbacks. Privacy, or lack thereof, was the first thing that came to mind. It would be limited, especially when church was in service. The entire congregation would be in the next room. She definitely couldn't skip church, not that she would anyway. She dared to guess that inevitably someone would come knocking on her door each week.

Abby's imagination ran through dozens of scenarios. A town resident might want to welcome her or a parent may wish to discuss a student. Perhaps an older child would think it funny to knock on her door and then run away. Privacy might very well be a thing of the past.

The idea of the Reverend being right outside of her room, various hours of both day and night, caused an uneasy feeling in Abby. Her past life flashed into her mind. She didn't deserve to live in a church, what if someone found out?

No, she told herself, she was forgiven and the past was over. She pushed the thoughts back, refusing to let them take control. She was far from Montana and Wesley Roberts. He would never find her and it was time for a fresh start.

The door hinge on the stagecoach squeaked loudly as the driver opened it. An older man with a long, grey beard popped his head inside the cabin, smiling as he spoke.

"We've arrived at Cedar Creek ma'am. I have your baggage unloaded and someone waiting to help you take it wherever you need it to go."

The older man held his hand out to the only passenger to take a hold. His voice sounded kind. "Can I help you down ma'am?" Abby was grateful for his offer and took the gentleman's assistance to step out of the stagecoach.

Once she was safely down, the driver went to tend to his horses. Abby knew they needed to be watered and deserved a good brush down after such a long trip.

After weeks of being jarred, bounced, and dusted, solid ground felt good under her feet. She was ready to get settled in her room at the church and freshen up.

Breathing in the crisp, clean air, honeysuckle and roses found their way into her senses. A smile lit her face, she could get used to this. What an ideal town, and a perfect place to live. She whispered a silent prayer of thanks to God for the new chapter about to begin in her life.

Her previous life was harsh, cruel in fact. Out of God's great mercy and compassion, He had rescued her and given her the innermost desires of her heart, a family. She was blessed with a mother, father, brother, sister-in-law, niece, and a baby niece or nephew on the way.

Now He was giving her the opportunity to help others learn and possibly assist in their spiritual eyes being opened. Most of her teaching lessons were gathered from the Bible. She found it an honor to use God's word to help others. It was a great way to effortlessly stay in the word each day.

Abby brushed the dust from her dress and composed herself. It had been a long few weeks. While viewing her surroundings, she noticed the dry goods store. A bar of lavender soap was what she needed. Fresh clothes and a warm bath would certainly make her feel as good as new. She decided as soon as she was unpacked, she would make her way back to the store for the soap.

A young boy, possibly sixteen, stood patiently by her luggage. He wore blue striped overalls with a red bandana hanging out of his back pocket. He had brown hair and freckles which made him appear childlike.

She motioned for him to come closer. "Hello, I am Miss Gibbs," she called out as the boy walked to where she stood. "I appreciate you helping me with my belongings today. I will be staying at the church. Would you deliver my things there?"

With a nod of his head, he replied with an enthusiastic voice. "Brandon Jennings, at your service ma'am. Yes, I will do it straight away."

Without another word, he tossed the strap of the smaller satchel bag over his shoulder. Firmly grasping the handle of the large trunk, he began to drag it down the dirt road toward the church.

Abby cringed, knowing the trunk would be torn to shreds if it was pulled across sharp rocks, and who knows what else, all the way to the church.

The trunk belonged to her adopted mother, Grace, who loaned it to Abby to use on her trip. It had been in the family for generations and was passed to Grace many years ago by her mother. It was a family treasure and of great sentimental value.

"Hold on, wait a minute," Abby called out. She hurried to catch then young man. Brandon stopped, looking back to see the new teacher approaching.

"I appreciate your help, but is there any other way that you can get my trunk to the church without dragging it?"

"No ma'am. It's too heavy to carry and I don't own a horse or wagon." He let loose of the trunk, causing the heavy chest to land on the ground with a thud, kicking up a brown cloud of dust.

"What if we both take a handle? We could carry it together." She wasn't at all sure if she could lift it, but she aimed to try.

"Yes ma'am, we can surely do that." Brandon again placed his hand on one of the handles. Abby placed a firm grip on the other side.

"Ready, set, go," she called out. Brandon lifted his end effortlessly. Abby managed to raise her side about a foot off of the ground. Slowly they began to inch forward. They weren't making much progress because Abby found the trunk to be much heavier than she had expected.

"Do you need to stop ma'am?" Brandon asked. Abby knew he could tell it put a strain on her but was determined not to give up.

"No thank you. I may have to take it slow, but am confident we can make it." She had a tinge of guilt not telling the truth. She wasn't sure at all. In fact, she didn't feel she could make it at all.

From the stagecoach, the church looked so beautiful perched on top of the little hill. Now Abby thought it looked a hundred grueling miles away. Within only a few more steps her strength began to fail. Her grip grew weak and arms began to shake. What was she going to do?

***

Across the street, at the Cedar Creek Jail, Sheriff Joshua Cole watched the two young people. He was slightly amused by the petite woman who struggled with the large trunk. They appeared to be trying to carry it down the street and out of town.

Josh recognized Brandon Jennings, but the woman was a stranger to him. He knew everyone and everything that went on in Cedar Creek. This led him to one conclusion. The young lady must be the new teacher, who was supposed to have come in on the noon stage.

Josh thought it silly that any woman would risk hurting herself or breaking her back, rather than get a single scratch on a meaningless old trunk. He hadn't formally met her but knew the type, a spoiled princess. He was sure she was accustomed to always getting things her way.

He'd heard that her father, John Gibbs, was a wealthy rancher. Miss Gibbs was undoubtably a self-centered rich kid, a rotten brat. In fact, Josh was positive of it. The more he thought about it, the more it irritated him. She probably never had a care in her life. Material things were what mattered the most to her. She probably never had to work a day in her life.

Josh looked down at the dog who sat at his feet. His faithful companion's big, brown eyes looked back at him. "Do you see that boy?" Max tilted his head to the side, as if listening intently to his master, and wagged his tail.

"Not one person in Cedar Creek has offered to lift a finger to help those two with that trunk." This set a burr under his tail feathers. He prided himself on the friendliness of his town. Cedar Creek was a welcoming place with pleasant people. It didn't matter how spoiled this woman was, she was still a lady who required assistance.

"Max, let's go boy! We have to defend the towns honor." With wag of his tail, the scruffy, big, salt and pepper colored dog happily joined his master. Out the door of the jail they marched.

Josh strode past the spectators, with Max close by his side. The sheriff cast a look of shame upon each of them as he went. He decided that he would address this matter later with the citizens. One should always lend a helping hand to those in need, not just stand idly by gawking.

Being a man of faith with a good heart, he could tolerate a lot and rarely lost his temper. Josh was known to be a fair man who hated rudeness, cruelty and lawlessness.

As his eyes met the gazes of those watching, they knew that he was ashamed of them, and rightfully so. Josh knew they didn't mean any harm, but was disappointed in their actions anyway.

***

"Excuse me Miss, let me help you with that." A man in his mid-twenties appeared in front of Abby. He was average height, had a well-trimmed beard, dark brown eyes and hair. He was accompanied by a large dog. Reaching around her, he took the handle out of her hands, allowing him to easily lift the chest.

Abby wasn't sure if she could have taken even one more step and was very relieved and thankful that someone offered to help. As the two men were depositing her belongings at the church, the worn-out woman sank onto the nearest bench.

Her new life adventure was not starting out so well. A few loose strands of her brown hair blew in the warm August breeze. She carefully swiped them away from her face, pulling them up, and neatly tucking them back into her bonnet.

A deep voice broke the silence, sounding from over her head. "Reverend Johnson put your things in your room at the church. He said to tell you that he had a few matters to attend to this afternoon, but he is most anxious to meet you." Glancing up, Abby peered into the dark brown eyes of the man who had come to her rescue.

"I'm Sheriff Joshua Cole, ma'am, and you are the new teacher?" The dark eyed man had an amused smile on his bearded face. Abby thought it not very nice to find her situation and weakness funny. The shiny gold star on his vest glistened as the sun hit it, reflecting light into Abby's eyes, which caused her to briefly look away.

Not wanting the sheriff to think her rude, she risked the sun's glare and looked back at the gentleman with smirky smile. She wasn't at all sure if this was someone that she was going to like. Avoiding the reflection of the tin star on his vest, Abby replied with kindness.

"You are correct, I am the new teacher in Cedar Creek, Miss Gibbs. It is a pleasure to meet you Sheriff. I want to express my sincere gratitude to you for taking my things to the church."

"I apologize to rush off so fast, but I have to check on a prisoner. If you need anything please don't hesitate to ask. You can find me in my office most days and nights ma'am."

To Abby's disappointment, with a tip of his hat, the sheriff and the big dog were gone in a flash. Not a welcome greeting of any kind. Not a "welcome to town," or "I hope you enjoy living in Cedar Creek." Nothing!

Sitting alone with her thoughts, feeling lost and unwelcome, she looked around. The boardwalk was clear of every living soul with the exception of her. Embarrassment filled her. She must have appeared awful to anyone who saw her. Stooped over, trying to hold up a giant trunk, her hair was unkempt, she was wearing a dirty dress and possibly not smelling the best. Not a good first impression at all.

Deciding that feeling sorry for herself wouldn't do any good she focused on her much-needed bath. The Reverend was busy, so she didn't have to hurry to the church. Soaking in warm water would surely make her feel better.

Standing, she set a course for the dry goods store. When she reached the window of the general store, she paused to look at the fine items in the window dressing.

A wooden woman manikin stood wearing a beautiful green dress. It was a simple fabric, light green colored cotton, with a yellow flowery print. Placing a hand to her neck, she felt the soft scarf that she wore almost every day.

It was the one thing from her past that was good, the first gift ever given to her. And making it more special was it came from her only friend at the time. It was a priceless, non-replaceable treasure.

The dress in the widow reminded her of the scarf and she loved it. Admiring the rest of the things placed nearby, Abby knew whoever had arranged it all had remarkable talent and fine taste.

Placing her hand on the knob, she opened the door ready to see what she could find inside to spark her interest, mainly a bar of soap. A tiny bell sounded as she closed the door behind herself. A young, beautiful girl with jet black hair and big blue eyes looked up from the counter. Her voice matched her well. A soft sweet tone called across the room to Abby.

"Hello, can I help you find anything Miss?" The attractive woman approached Abby wearing a beaming smile. As the clerk neared, Abby could tell that the woman was tall, possibly five foot nine. Abby was short, only five foot two inches. She didn't normally mind but watching the graceful movements of the blue-eyed beauty sparked a bit of jealousy.

Abby was simple, ordinary, a plain Jane in fact. That's what Wesley always called her. Hurt pierced her heart as thoughts of the horrid man rushed in. Not wanting any more memories of him to invade her mind, she quickly engaged in conversation.

"Yes, do you carry lavender soap? I have had a very long stage ride and I am in desperate need of it." Well, that didn't sound very nice, Abby thought, immediately regretting her choice of words. I just told a woman whom I don't know that

I am the smelly new girl. Just great! That's when she noticed, the beauty queen had an odd look on her face, the same as did the sheriff. She was beginning to think that this town wasn't so perfect after all.

Turning, the tall woman walked across the room to a shelf housing several personal care items. Abby could see hair combs, brushes, a small silver mirror, and a bottle of perfume. Retrieving something from the collection of items, she gracefully, almost floated across the floor back to her customer.

"Here you go hon," as she offered a bright smile. "Is there anything else you need?" The clerk held out a large fragrant bar of lavender soap in her hand. Abby couldn't help but wonder if this was a flawless woman, attractive and sweet? She felt more minuscule by the moment.

Collecting the soap from the other woman's hand, her insides jumped for joy. It had been ages since her last bath. "Thank you, this is all I need for today. How much do I owe you?" Abby reached into her pocket-sized money purse, that was looped around her wrist.

The other woman held up a hand in protest. "I'll put it on your tab. You can settle up another day. I'm sure you will be needing other things later, when you get settled in."

"My tab? What tab?"

"You're the new teacher. It's all over town that you arrived on the noon stage today. Oh dear, I'm dreadfully sorry. How rude of me. I'm Rebecca Anderson. My father owns the store. I help by tending the counter and with all of the lady's items.

My mother Sarah, owns the diner, Anderson Café. My brother Randy is the deputy. So, you will see my entire family a lot," she spoke with a chuckle.

Rebecca appeared to be a truly nice person. Not knowing anyone in town, perhaps the lady clerk would be a friend to Abby, she hoped this would be the case.

"It is a pleasure to meet you Miss Anderson. I am Miss Gibbs and the teacher as you guessed. Please call me Abby. Cedar Creek is a very charming town. I look forward to meeting and getting to know the local people." Abby offered a timid smile.

"Yes, please put the soap on my tab. I appreciate your kindness. I am quite weary. It's been such a long, tedious trip and I certainly could use a bath." Abby cringed over her poor choice of words again. Maybe someday she would look back on herself saying that she was the smelly girl and laugh, but not today.

Abby chatted with Rebecca a few more minutes, then excused herself. She wanted that bath desperately, and a good night's sleep and it was getting late. Pulling the door of the mercantile closed, she paused outside the store to smell her fragrant bar of soap.

Out of nowhere, a man shot past her in a dead run, hitting the corner of her shoulder. The soap flew from her fingers, landing a few feet away on the boardwalk.

Suddenly the sheriff appeared, his gun drawn, ready to fire. His long legs ate up the distance as he rushed up the boardwalk in the direction of the first man. Before Abby could retrieve the soap, the sheriff's boot stomped down on it. The soap skidded away, causing the man's foot to slip out from underneath him, sending him crashing down onto the boardwalk. The fleeing man vanished quickly from sight.

Sheriff Cole lay flat on his back. Abby rushed to his side. His eyes where closed and he wasn't moving. What was she going to do? Her heart began to race, what if the sheriff was dead?

Chapter 2

Wesley hurried to pack his bags but spotted the crumpled letter that he had received from the detective, laying on the floor. Snatching it up with his right hand, he paused to scan the note once more, having read it a dozen times already. Each time fueled a bitter anger that had been building for years.

> Dear Mr. Roberts,
> It is with great pleasure that I write to you today. I have at long last located the girl whom you seek, Abby Mathews. She has been living in Montana with a family by the name of Gibbs.
> After further investigation it was discovered that John Gibbs, a

wealthy rancher, adopted Miss Mathews five years ago. She has been residing at the Gibbs ranch, using her new name, Abby Gibbs, since her adoption.

Also living on the ranch is John's wife Grace and her son from a previous marriage, Dakota Russell. Mr. Gibbs adopted Grace's son Dakota, as well, when he was a young boy, having no biological children of his own.

I took it upon myself to visit the family residence, under false pretenses of course. I told the family that I was interested in purchasing a prize bull that was for sale and wished to see it.

It was then that I discovered that Miss Gibbs was leaving on the next stagecoach for Cedar Creek, Missouri, where she is to become the new school teacher.

There is no further information available at this time. I am glad to have been of assistance to you in finding your missing person.

If you are ever to need my services again, please do not hesitate to contact me.

Sincerely
James Rinker, Rinker Investigation Services.

"I will find you Abby, and when I do…" With a tight-fisted grip, Wesley crumbed the letter in his hand. Wadding it into a tight little ball, he harshly threw it into the metal trash can that sat on the floor beside his desk.

Opening a drawer, he took out a match, striking it on the side of the box. He let it purposely fall from his fingers into the can, causing the paper to quickly catch on fire. As it rapidly burned, he gazed into the flames.

"Enjoy your freedom while it lasts, my little runaway. When I find you, and I will, you're going to wish that you had never been born! Years of hard work, destroyed in a single moment. I almost lost everything because of you and I intend to see that you suffer because of it."

"No one betrays Wesley Roberts, especially a worthless female. Double crossing me was a deadly mistake." He placed a finger on his chin, in thought.

"Granted, I do now have a much larger, more valuable saloon and brothel. But I will not tolerate the treachery of anyone, especially a wretched female. That woman will learn her place." A partial smile lit his face.

"Maybe I shouldn't kill her too fast. I'm sure that I can find ways to teach her a lesson for what she's done and enjoy doing it. I can always use an extra girl in my brothel. Men will devour a young girl and pay a pretty penny to do it." Laughter escaped his lips. Watching the fire, Wesley soon found himself remembering back, all those years ago.

***

A knock was heard at the front door of the saloon at sunrise. "Who would get a man out of bed at this time of day?" Wesley grumbled as he stomped down the hall to answer the door.

Everything after that happened so fast it was a blur. Four men pushed past him, saying they were there to collect his assets. Wesley had purchased many expensive items on credit and had no funds to pay for them.

New gambling tables, a fine carriage with a strong horse team to pull it, new tailored silk shirts, furniture, cigars, and several other things were all collected.

He watched powerlessly as he was stripped of all his possessions. The Roberts Saloon, Roberts Title and Deed Company, his horse, and all the expensive clothing he owned. Even Anna Bell, his only lady of the evening, was collected as partial payment for his debt.

Every single thing he owned was taken away. As the sun set that day, all Wesley had left was the shirt on his back and ten dollars that was hidden inside his boot.

The first few days after his downfall were harsh. Lack of food, lodging, and loss of dignity plagued him. But as fate would have it, on the third day, his luck changed. Hungry and dirty he wandered into a miner's camp looking for a handout of food and drink.

"I have never had to beg before." Wesley growled under his breath, anger clearly building in his face.

Several of the miners in camp were in a heated poker game. They were loud and clearly drunk. There was a huge gold strike earlier that day. Everyone was celebrating by drinking heavily, gambling, and tossing gold nuggets around as if they were ordinary rocks. It didn't seem to matter to the intoxicated men how careless they were with their new-found riches.

"What luck." Wesley grew excited. He was a master at cards and cheating at poker. It took him mere minutes to worm his way into a card game, and even less time to win every gold nugget of each player.

He was calm and wise with every win, slowly pocketing the money, not flashing his winnings. He kept only a few dollars on the table at a time. Fortunately, the miners were so drunk they didn't notice as Wesley helped himself to anything of value he wanted.

Deep into the night, everyone was passed out in a drunken stupor except Wesley. He located two of the best horses without any identifiably markings, not wanting to be caught and hung as a horse thief. He swiftly stuffed as many saddle bags with as much gold and valuables as each horse could carry. Under the cover of darkness, he promptly rode away into the night a very wealthy man. Leaving Montana, he headed for the land of opportunity, California.

Once there, he put his ill-gotten riches to work. After a few years it all paid off for him. He was the owner of several small businesses, Roberts Bank, Roberts Fine Jewelry and the largest brothel for miles around, Roberts Saloon Hall with Gambling and Girls. His wealth had increased immensely. He was living on top of the world.

One day he saw an ad for the Rinker Detective Agency. "I wonder if they could find Abby Mathews?" Wesley pondered out loud. "I haven't forgotten you my dear. I crave your blood, your soul." The more he spoke, the darker his voice grew.

"It may be a waste of my money, but I crave revenge more." That day he contacted the agency, hiring them regardless of their fee.

***

The paper was completely burned up. There were only a few smoldering ashes that remained. Fueled by angry memories, thoughts began to vocally roll from his lips.

"What shall I do first when I find you? Toss you to the flesh devouring men at the brothel or ravage you myself? Maybe I should skin you alive or break each of your thieving little fingers?"

Grabbing the whip that was always kept nearby, for teaching lessons, he snapped it through the air. The leather slapped against the corner of the desk, leaving a mark. With brute force, he savagely struck the desk repeatedly, like an out of control animal. His face turned red and sweat beaded up on his forehead.

More memories flooded him. "I was to become rich that day, beyond my wildest dreams. I had made plans for weeks."

His face grew tight, his eyes narrowed. "Then out of nowhere that stranger burst into my office, offering to buy both girls, Elizabeth and Abby. I should have shot him on the spot and kept the money and the women."

Wesley's eyes grew dark. "He tossed all those gold nuggets at my feet, tantalizing me. How was I supposed to know it was a trick, only fool's gold? Abby, you won't escape me again."

You will taste my leather," he yelled like a roaring lion. "I will beat you without mercy until you scream." With a hard snap of his wrist he threw the whip across the room. Turning around with a clenched tight fist, he punched the wall, but immediately drew it back.

Various curses flew from his mouth as he cradled his hand. After several minutes of foul language, he inspected himself for any injury or broken bones.

"This is going to be black and blue by tomorrow. That woman isn't here and she's causing me pain. Why do I let her get under my skin so bad? Calm down Wesley. Revenge is at your fingertips. She can't escape you for much longer. There's nowhere to run, she can't hide."

His features gradually returned to normal. His usual calm composure was again in place. Noticing his reflection in the window glass, he studied himself. What he saw looking back was a tall man with black hair, blue eyes, a chiseled jaw line, broad shoulders and muscular body.

"Look at yourself. You're a handsome man, and a wealthy one. You have women throwing themselves at your feet, yet you couldn't control one petite little girl. Are you losing your touch? No, I'm a good man and she wasn't worthy of me." he assured himself.

"I don't understand why that girl didn't appreciate all the things I did for her? I took her in as an orphan, fed and clothed her. She was fortunate to have me."

"I protected her and didn't let another man touch her. Why wasn't she grateful? Everything I did was for her own good. I had to use the belt or whip. It was my duty as a man, to teach her to be submissive and to please me. A good man teaches women their place. I am indeed a good man."

Smoothing out the collar on his shirt Wesley turned away from his reflection and returned to his packing. It didn't take long before he was ready to leave. Walking out the door, he headed for his horse. Mounting up, Wesley slapped the reins down hard on the side of his black stallion.

"Yaw horse," he called out. "Cedar Creek, vengeance is coming to town and he's not leaving alone."

Chapter 3

"Sheriff! Sheriff Cole! Can you hear me?" Abby franticly called out, "Please God, don't let me have killed the sheriff." Kneeling down beside him on the walkway, using both of her hands she grabbed one of Josh's shoulders and began to shake him. Receiving no response, she continued to shake him a bit harder. To her dismay, he remained motionless with his eyes closed.

The entire town seemed to be deserted, strangely not a soul was in sight. She wanted the sheriff to wake up desperately. If she could not revive him soon, she would have to find help. Before her thoughts could travel any further, a large shaggy dog appeared beside her. It was the same one that she had seen earlier with Sheriff Cole. It stood peering down at the motionless man for a moment.

Unexpectedly the dog lowered its head down to his masters and began to lick him on the face. Abby watched as he began to paw at his owner's arm. She thought it touching how the animal seemed to be expressing love and concern to his owner. Gently she pushed the canine away, knowing that a lick in the face wasn't an ideal wake up call.

"I know boy, I'm worried too." Abby spoke uplifting words but knew something had to be done to help the sheriff. Turning to God, she prayed.

"Lord, please watch over the sheriff. Protect him from being hurt or injured in any way and certainly not be dead. I want to thank you for hearing my prayer. I know you have this under control. Amen." With a small whimper the dog sat down near his master.

"Don't worry boy, he will be okay." Abby reached over and patted the shaggy animals head softly. Looking back at the man who lay on the ground, there was not any sign of life. Abby leaned her head down, placing it upon his chest. If she could hear a heartbeat or perhaps feel the rise and fall of his breathing, she would not worry as much.

Her bonnet covered her ear, making it hard to hear anything. Rushing to untie it, she flung it off, letting her long brown hair fall across her shoulders. She quickly placed her ear back on the man's chest. Still, not a sound could be heard. Maybe his vest was in the way? It was made of thick leather, which might make it harder to hear. Rapidly, she pulled the vest apart, listening once more. To her relief, she heard a heartbeat.

***

Suddenly, Josh was aware that something was on top of him. Instinctively his hands and arms flung around the object. He wasn't sure what had happened, if he was being attacked, robbed or if the escaped prisoner was trying to kill him.

What he did know was that he was not going down without a fight. His eyes flashed open as his hands made contact with his assailant. The sheriff's grip was tight, strong, and it hurt Abby.

Josh was suddenly face to face with a mass of long brown hair. His eyes were met with the soft, brown eyes and the most beautiful smile that he had ever seen. Was he dead and this an angel?

Catching Josh off guard, the angel began to scream. He sprang to his feet, tossing the pretty angel backward. That's when he realized that he had just thrown the new teacher bouncing down the boardwalk.

Remembering the fleeing prisoner, Josh swiftly scanned the area for any danger. Once his surroundings were secure, he gently helped Miss Gibbs up.

Max had rushed to Josh's side, with his tail wagging. The big dog was more than a loyal companion, he was a friend with four legs. Josh patted the animal's back with long smooth easy movements, causing loose fur to fall to the ground. Max had a soothing effect on his owner.

"What happened? How long was I out and why do I smell lavender?"

"Are you injured? I'm very sorry this happened. It is somewhat my fault. I should not have stopped in the middle of the walkway to smell my soap. When that man rushed by me, he hit my shoulder causing my bar of soap to drop out of my hands. Before I could pick it back up, you slipped on it and fell. I'm truly sorry sheriff." Abby held her head down as she spoke, feeling sincerely remorseful.

Josh couldn't help but be slightly distracted. How had he not noticed how pretty she was earlier, when they had first met that day? How small and dainty Miss Gibbs was and very lovely....

What was he doing? Shake it off Josh.... You don't need to get involved with a woman right now. You have a town to run and criminals to catch. It's a life for a single man. Besides, he assured himself, Miss Gibbs was accustomed to expensive homes, fine clothes and was spoiled. He didn't want a selfish bratty woman.

"Why were you on top of me?" Did you have to ask her that? Josh wished he hadn't blurted out what was in his head so fast, until he saw the heat fill her cheeks. Now this, Josh thought, might be fun after all. The little lady was blushing. He couldn't help but smile back at her.

Angelic brown eyes stared back at him. Josh liked how her long, shiny hair framed her face as it fell across her shoulders. Her skin looked creamy soft and her lips were red as roses.

"I was not on top of you sir. I can assure you." The feisty woman fired back with dignity. "I was merely listening to see if you had a heartbeat. You gave me a terrible fright." She placed a hand on her heart in gesture, only to feel her hair dangling wild and unrestrained.

More heat filled her cheeks as she hurriedly collected her bonnet, putting it on and shoving her hair up underneath it as fast as her tiny hands would allow. Josh knew that she was embarrassed. She sure was a pretty thing, especially when she blushed.

Footsteps brought Josh's head up, away from his angel. Randy, his deputy, was coming up the walkway with the escaped prisoner in handcuffs beside him. Max was at his side, panting heavily. Josh had been so captivated by the new teacher, he hadn't realized his dog was gone.

"Sheriff, I... Well, your dog and me, caught this low-down scoundrel trying to sneak out of town. I spotted Max scratching at the blacksmiths back door. I knew something was amiss. That's when this rascal jumped out of the side window and took off on foot."

"He must have been trying to wait until dark so he could sneak away without being seen. But good 'ole Max flushed him out and then chased him down." Randy filled the sheriff in on all of the details. Pausing as if just noticing the girl, Randy looked at Josh and then at Abby with amusement.

Josh knew that look. Randy had seen too much, he could read the sheriff like an open book. Josh didn't aim to explain the heat in Miss Gibb's face or the big smile on his. Trying to get his deputy's mind on something else he hurried to speak.

"Good Job Deputy Anderson. I was in pursuit when I had an unforeseen accident." Josh looked right into Abby's eyes. "I was ambushed by a bar of soap." Josh gave Abby a wink.

"What?" Randy looked confused. "How could a bar of soap attack a fella?" Josh didn't want to take the time to explain and he wasn't going to wait around for Randy to start asking other questions, particularly ones about the pretty new teacher.

Randy loved flirting with the ladies, and the ladies seemed to flock to him, like bees to honey. Feeling a tinge of jealousy, Josh hoped that this was one woman that Randy would leave alone.

Josh decided that he had better shake off the thoughts about this woman and get back to work. Springing into action, Josh forcefully grabbed the prisoner by his arm and set a course for the jail. The sheriff motioned for his deputy to follow along, not wanting to give Randy an opportunity to pour out the charm on Miss Gibbs.

"Deputy Anderson, are you coming? We have a town to protect." Josh gave a whistle and Max joined him. Deputy Anderson paused to tip his hat at Abby, then left in a rush to catch up with the sheriff.

Abby watched as the two brave, nice looking men walked away. Shocked at her thoughts, she scolded herself in a whisper.

"Abby you know that men are dangerous, even deadly. Why would you look twice at a man, ever? You're finally free, happy, and can hold your head up. Stay away from men!"

***

Randy locked the door to the cell of the recaptured horse thief. Turning, he tossed the keys onto his sheriff's desk, then began his inquiry.

"So, Sheriff Cole, what happed back there? Hum…?" A grin lit his face as he added to his questioning. "More importantly, why did you look so smitten? I've never seen that look on your face before. Not ever, even around Rebecca."

"What look, I didn't have any look?" Josh had to be careful how he answered and be sure to control his facial expressions. He wasn't going to let Randy get him into trouble. Randy had a way of getting Josh in messes and caused him problems in the past. Randy, being childish at times, loved dares and bets and always found a way to get Josh involved.

One dare in particular stood out, the church picnic last summer. Every detail of the awful day flooded out of Josh's memory filling his thoughts. The day ended with Josh eating a worm. His stomach churned just thinking of it. He was not about to let Randy trick him into another dare or a bet. He refused to let his deputy twist his words. He would stand firm and hold his ground, he hoped.

"Are you listening to me?" Randy's voice brought Josh's thoughts back to the problem at hand, a nosy deputy. "I saw that big 'ole grin and the wink that you gave that teacher. If that isn't flirting, then I don't know what is. Are you going to ask her to dinner sometime?"

"Why would I do that? She's not my type," Josh said in a nonchalant tone.

"What type is that sheriff? The pretty, petite type? Or maybe it's the type of woman who has a brain? I know you can't stand a woman who can think for herself." Josh had mentioned to Randy many times that he wanted a smart, sensible woman. Besides being childish, Josh thought Randy was a master at sarcasm.

"No" said Josh, "the type that's been spoiled all of her life. The type who is selfish and feels entitled to anything she wants. And to top it off, she's clumsy. She almost killed me with that bar of soap. I have no intention of courting her, so drop it Randy."

"Touchy, touchy. If you're not interested in her, then you won't mind if I pursue the brown eyed beauty?" Randy smiled playfully.

Josh knew his deputy was up to something, and it probably wasn't good. Not that Randy was a bad sort of fella, because he wasn't. He was the best deputy and friend that a sheriff could ask for, with the exception of the pranks and dares. Randy was hard working, loyal, and had Josh's back in a pinch. Most importantly he liked Max.

As much as Josh didn't want to let Randy push his buttons, his deputy was succeeding in whatever plot he was cooking up. Josh felt jealous and slightly mad, both of which, he was ashamed to admit.

Miss Gibbs was pretty and smart, qualities that he found desirable in a wife. Wife? How had he gone from thinking that a woman was pretty, to using the word wife? Josh scolded himself, he didn't want to get married. He didn't like the new teacher anyway, did he? No. No, of course not. A spoiled rich girl. Absolutely not!

Josh thought a moment longer, he didn't want Randy to court her either though. Randy liked to kiss and tell. He had ruined more than one woman's reputation. Granted the women shouldn't have been kissing him, but a gentleman would not have spread it all over town.

Josh remembered the look that he saw in Abby's eyes. Something was different in that girl's eyes, but he wasn't sure what? It was almost as if she carried both a fear and a deep sadness at the same time. Walking to the jailhouse window, Josh stared outside.

Blankly looking off into space, debating on what his true thoughts were toward Miss Gibbs. After all, he didn't know her, how could he have feelings for her? Movement caught his attention. Max was across the street sitting on the walkway wagging his tail. Josh followed Max's gaze and saw Miss Gibbs walking directly toward his dog. Being highly protective of Max, Josh's senses became instantly heighted.

As the woman approached, Max sprang up. He took off in a slow jog to meet her. Without warning he jumped up, putting his front two paws on her shoulders and began to lick her face. He was as tall as she was when he stood up on his two hind legs. Josh was surprised that the big animal didn't knock her down.

As she was being licked, Miss Gibbs began laughing, to Josh's amazement. Any other person would not have been very thrilled with doggie kisses. Miss Gibbs giggled and rubbed Max's head and his back. Josh had never seen his dog's tail wag so fast. The silly animal seemed to be smitten for the teacher too.

Feeling torn, Josh wondered why he had to witness any of that? How could this woman melt his heart so fast? She had only been in town a matter of hours and he couldn't shake her from his mind.

If Randy decided to pursue her, he would not appreciate her inelegance or her obvious love for animals. Would he ruin her reputation, or more importantly, would she let him kiss her?

Josh didn't like that thought. He didn't want Randy to kiss her, ever. The same jealous feelings that he had felt earlier resurfaced. Now he had to decide what he was going to do about them?

Calling on her one time couldn't hurt anything, could it? As sheriff, it was his job to welcome new people to town and show them around. Yes, that would be his excuse to visit the pretty lady tomorrow. Now his only problem was how to handle his snoopy deputy? Turning back toward his deputy, Josh noticed Randy was also looking out the window at Miss Gibbs.

"She wouldn't want a guy like you. You're right, not to ask her out." Randy broke the silence in the room.

"What do you mean a guy like me? I could call on her if I wanted to."

"Of course, you can," Randy snickered sarcastically. "Besides, it wouldn't be your fault if she turned you down, a snooty female like her. A sheriff's wages wouldn't satisfy her, being accustomed to fine things and all."

What Randy said was all true. He couldn't afford to give her a life of wealth. Why did he care anyway? He didn't know the woman and was already thinking about how he could not afford her. This was all Randy's doing, putting ideas in his head. Well, he wasn't going to fall for it!

"I think I might pay the new teacher a visit later. Maybe I'll show her around town and then take her to mom's dinner for a bite to eat." The deputy's mother owned the only eating place in Cedar Creek, Anderson's Café. Randy would take the women he was courting there to eat and didn't have to pay a dime. A real cheapskate, Josh thought.

"I bet she would prefer me over you? My family owns half of the town. I'm more in her league."

That did it, Josh was all out angry. Randy was not by any stretch of the word, above him. The more he thought of Miss Gibbs being kissed by another man, the more it bothered him.

"I think I will go calling on the teacher real soon." Randy smiled at Josh. Now what? If Randy takes her out, he will over exaggerate anything and everything. It won't be long and the entire town will think Miss Gibbs a tainted woman.

Josh wrestled with his thoughts a few more minutes, but knew what he had to do. Everything inside of him screamed, protect Miss Gibbs! Though Randy may embellish the truth, he wasn't dangerous. Yet something deep inside of Josh knew this woman was in immense danger and he was her only hope.

Chapter 4

Reverend Johnson wasn't at all what Abby expected. She had imagined an old, short, heavy set, gentleman whose belly jiggled when he laughed. Instead he appeared to be in his mid-fifties and fairly tall, over six-foot Abby guessed. He had a friendliness about him that made her feel at ease and calm. It was almost as if she had known him all of her life.

He had greeted her with a welcoming smile and a firm hand shake. He insisted she call him R.J., short for Reverend Johnson. In mere minutes of their conversation, Abby could tell that he loved the Lord with all his heart. He spoke with a passion for

God. It made her look forward to hearing his sermon on Sunday.

Smiling as they walked, the Pastor gave her the grand tour of the entire church. It consisted of only two rooms. The larger, main room was where the church services were held and school was to be taught. The second, and only other room, was hers.

The older gentleman was very chatty, which normally wasn't a bad thing, but feeling exhausted won over socializing in Abby's mind. She was relieved when he finally dismissed himself to go home for supper. He said his wife, Martha, was a stickler for having food on the table at five o'clock sharp.

He insisted that Abby join his wife and himself for their evening meal. Abby had thanked him but politely declined. She explained that she wanted to get settled and was tired but would love to join them another time.

At long last Abby was alone. She eagerly opened the wooden plank door which led to her living quarters. The hinges squeaked slightly upon opening as she stepped into the doorway. She paused to observe each detail of her new home.

To her right sat a single narrow bed. Two flat boards were nailed together to form an L shaped shelf headboard. This would be a perfect spot for her Bible and a candle, she thought. The bed was made with the most beautiful quilt that Abby had ever seen.

Pastor Johnson had explained how several women from church had gotten together and made the quilt especially for her. Each block consisted of a flower which was designed by a different lady.

Abby smiled, it made her bed look like a flower garden of fabric. Every detail was masterfully planned out, a beautiful work of art in her eyes. She made a mental note to personally thank each woman responsible.

A rope was hung diagonally, stretching from corner to corner, a few feet past the bed. This would be a good place to hang her dresses out to dry on wash day. She only had three, but she didn't feel the need for more.

Two dresses for everyday wear. The third, a nicer dress, was for church and special occasions. Next to the edge of the rope, on the adjoining wall beside her bed, stood a small three drawer dresser. A cream-colored water pitcher and bowl stood on top of it.

Abby's heart jumped for joy when she spotted the round wash tub next to the dresser. She guessed it was barely big enough for her to sit down inside it. She didn't mind though, it would do the job. The next wall housed a window and another door that led outside. Abby was delighted to have her own private entrance.

Pale green cotton curtains hung from the single pane window. Below it sat a small writing desk, with one drawer. Sitting on top was a candle and writing paper. Standing in front of the last wall of her room was a black cast iron stove and a wood box filled with wood.

A grey metal bucket sat empty nearby. She would use it to heat the water for her bath once a fire was built. It would make her room muggy hot but a refreshing bath was worth it.

Peeking out the window, she noticed a narrow brook which ran close by the church. It flowed gently down the hillside, straight into the waterwheel at the sawmill.

"Fresh water for a bath!" Delighted, Abby collected the bucket and hurried outside to the brook. Scooping up her first pail of water, she rushed back inside. After closing the door behind her, she sat the bucket down close by.

Opening the stove door to look inside, just as she suspected, it was ready to light. All she needed to do was start the fire. Looking around, she saw a box of matches lying on the floor beside the wood. Collecting it, she carefully pulled out a single match. Striking it, she easily lit the fire.

She placed the bucket on the stove to heat. While she waited, she decided to unpack her trunk which was sitting in the center of the room. She went to it, eager to put her things away.

Over the next thirty minutes she had emptied the hot steamy water into her tub and refilled it three times. At long last it was ready, Abby stepped into the wash tub. Warm, clean water touched her toes. The water felt wonderful. Slowly she lowered herself down to sit. She placed her legs over the side, making it possible to rest her back on the wall of the tub. As the steamy water flowed over her, she let her eyes close in total relaxation.

After about ten minutes of soaking, she remembered the soap that she had earlier placed on the dresser. Thinking it was not close enough to reach without getting up, she stretched as far as her arm could reach. Her fingers could almost grasp the lavender soap.

Suddenly a loud sound startled her. She had accidently knocked her hand-held mirror off the dresser, sending it crashing to the floor. Grasping it quickly, she prayed that it wasn't broke, it being the only mirror she had. Pulling it to her face she examined it for any damage. It had miraculously survived the fall without so much as a scratch.

As she peered at her refection, she worried. Did people know about her past? What if they found out? Maybe that's why the sheriff and Rebecca had looked at her oddly? Her mind started to go down a dark path. She forced herself to lay the mirror down and pray.

"Lord, I know I am forgiven and the things that happened all those years ago were not my fault. I was only a child, but why do I feel so ashamed and have so much trouble forgiving myself? Please help me to put the past behind me for good. Your word says, who the Son sets free is free indeed. I must remember that I am free!" Praying soothed her. Keeping her eyes closed she soaked a while longer.

***

Josh studied the paper in his hand. It was already dark and the Reverend had probably left the church for the night. He had promised to have a copy of his justice of the peace license on R.J.'s desk by morning, and he intended to keep that promise.

R.J. was leaving for an important trip, at five a.m., to Forsyth, Missouri. A meeting was being held to select a collection of ten pastors from various churches around the state, to be sent out to evangelize in the bigger towns. The counsel thought it more effective and safer to send a group of men.

Reverend Johnson told Josh that he wanted to preach locally and wasn't thrilled about being sent away from Martha, but felt if God led him there, he would go. Josh was proud of his pastor, who was willing to put God's will above his own desires.

To be eligible, each pastor must provide proof that a minister or justice of the peace was in the area to serve as their replacement. The mission's counsel viewed it of great importance for communities to have someone to preform marriages or provide counseling. Looking at the licensee that he held in his hand, he knew he couldn't let R.J. down.

"Max, stay here boy. I won't be long." The sleepy dog opened his eyes to acknowledge hearing his master's voice. As if knowing every word Josh said, the tired dog yawned and closed his eyes again.

Josh laughed, "Don't let me interrupt your beauty sleep boy." With a firm grip on the paper, Josh headed out the door, heading straight for the Reverend's office.

A soft light shown from the church, like a beacon in the night. It was coming from Miss Gibbs room. Josh wondered why she was up this late, but was glad she was. Maybe this would be his chance to get a step ahead of Randy, and ask her to have breakfast at the café with him. Nearing the church, a touch of nervousness struck him.

What if she said no? What if she really didn't like me at all? Josh tossed several more questions around until he realized that he was putting the cart before the horse. Why worry over something that hadn't happened?

The church doors were never locked. Josh walked in easily, going straight to the Reverend's modest desk, which sat in front of the room behind the pulpit. He placed the paper on top of R.J.'s Bible, knowing that it would undoubtedly be found right away. Now he was free to pursue other matters, a breakfast invitation to the new teacher.

The door to Miss Gibbs room was open about six inches. A narrow beam of light spilled into the otherwise darkened sanctuary. Josh took a deep breath and headed for the light. Pausing, he checked his shirt, making sure it was tucked in properly, straightened his hat, and then took a second big breath. One more step and he would be close enough to knock, then there would be no turning back.

Moving forward, Josh put his hand out to knock, but quickly pulled it back. He could see plainly right into Miss Gibbs room. What he saw caused him to look longer than he should have. Abby was sitting in a wash tub facing away from him. The only thing he could see was the top of her back and shoulders.

Numerous whelps and scars covered her skin. Some were raised and red, others thin and white. They not only covered her back but traveled over her shoulders. Josh couldn't help but wonder what would have scarred her skin like that?

Silently, he backed away. He was a man of God and didn't want to see anything that he shouldn't. He also didn't want to shame an innocent woman. It only took a minute for him to arrive back outside, on the church steps. He sat down, deciding to guard the door. Anyone could walk in, just as he had. Josh wanted to make sure that Miss Gibbs bath time remained private.

***

The morning air was brisk, with a brilliantly colorful sunrise. Josh loved early mornings, they were his favorite part of the day. On this day he was especially eager to begin his morning. Sipping the last few drops of his coffee, he placed the empty cup on his desk. It was almost seven a. m. and Miss Gibbs would be awake by now, any decent woman would be.

Summoning his nerve to go visit Miss Gibbs, he told Max to stay as he headed out the door. It was perfect weather for a hearty breakfast at the Café and then a leisurely carriage ride in the country.

A beaming smile spread across his face. He expected by lunchtime that a beautiful woman would be sitting in the buckboard seat beside him. A pleasant thought indeed.

His excitement quickly vanished as he looked ahead. Coming down the path, heading straight toward him was Randy with the teacher by his side. As they approached, Randy's smirk said it all.

"Good morning Sheriff. Miss Gibbs and I are going to the Café for breakfast. Then I'm going to show her around town. We would love for you join us, but I know you must have your morning rounds to make." With a tip of his hat and a sweet smile from Miss Gibbs the duo headed onward toward town.

Josh felt slightly jealous but refused to admit it. He told himself there would be other opportunities to call on Miss Gibbs. Randy couldn't do her reputation any harm at breakfast or on a tour of the town in broad daylight. Trying not to feel defeated, he proceeded to make his rounds as usual.

***

As any gentleman would, Deputy Anderson pulled the chair out for the lady, then seated himself. He then ordered coffee, blueberry muffins, scrambled eggs and bacon for them both. Abby liked all those foods but was irritated by not being allowed to order for herself.

Once the food arrived, she said a prayer of thanks, only to look up and see Randy had already eaten half of his breakfast. She was astonished at the deputy's rudeness and his shear disreguard for her prayer

Their breakfast came to an end, far too slowly for Abby. She knew this was not a man that she was interested in. Besides being rude, insensitive, and self-absorbed, he ate like a pig. Smacking his lips with each bite, and talking with his mouth full as he ate repulsed her.

When the self-absorbed man belched loudly without even an "Excuse me," flashes of an ugly past pushed its way into her conscience. Wesley told her what to eat, when to eat, and how much. If she was disobedient, the whip or belt was used.

Once, when she only fourteen, she was forced to sleep outside on the porch steps. Wesley said that's where dogs, like her, belonged. Abby hated remembering the past, and ran from it, but it always had a way to find her. It ate at her soul like a poison.

Abby wanted to run out of the room, this man brought too many horrid memories back, ones she wanted to fade away forever. Even after so many years had passed, each memory remained painfully vivid. Abby knew that Mr. Anderson was a decent man at heart, but not for her!

"Did you enjoy your meal ma'am?" Abby looked up to see Sheriff Cole smiling down at her.

"The food was delicious." It was all she could do not to add, but the company was terrible.

"She is having a grand time, who wouldn't with me as their escort?" Randy waved his coffee cup in the air at the waitress, "I need a refill over here."

"I just stopped by for one of Momma Anderson's famous cinnamon rolls. I didn't mean to intrude on your meal. I'll be on my way." He turned to walk away.

Grabbing the lawman's arm, almost in a panic, "No intrusion at all Sheriff Cole, please join us." She didn't want to spend one more second alone with his deputy. She needed to think of a way to excuse herself politely. Releasing her grip on the sheriff's arm she placed her hands in her lap.

Josh looked at her briefly, but Abby couldn't gauge his thoughts. "If you're sure I'm not intruding ma'am?" Abby breathed a sigh of relief when he agreed.

"Deputy Anderson, I've taken so much of your time today. Please don't let me keep you from your duties." Being polite and subtle at the same time, in her situation, was harder than she imagined. She apparently wasn't very good at either because the deputy continued to talk as if not hearing a word she spoke.

Trying once more, Abby interrupted Randy mid-sentence. Not a polite thing to do, but the man wouldn't give her a chance to talk otherwise.

"Deputy Anderson, your job has to be very demanding? It must take dedication to others and a lot of self-sacrifice on your part. I am feeling selfish keeping you so long when you have so many important things to do."

At this point, by the look on Josh's face, he must have picked up on the hints that she wanted away from Randy. The deputy was the only one oblivious to this fact as he kept on talking, about himself.

"You are right ma'am. Deputy Anderson is an invaluable asset to all the citizens of Cedar Creek. I don't know what I'd do without him. Which reminds me, Randy, will you run over to Mrs. Johnson's house? Find out if R.J. found the paperwork that I left for him this morning? And while you're there, find out if he was able to leave on time."

After a short pause he added, "I'm sorry to ask you to do it right now, but I'm headed out to the Franklin's place. I have to pick up my saddlebags and I'm running late already. We both know that a trip to the Johnson's is never a short one."

Looking toward Abby he added, "Billy Franklin is the best leather worker in the country and Mrs. Johnson won't let anyone leave without tea and cake." Giving Abby a wink, he added, "And I will make sure Miss Gibbs gets home safely"

Abby jumped up, grasping Josh's arm. "Thank you, Sheriff." Abby's heart flooded with relief. Turning to her host she added rapidly, "And thank you Mr. Anderson for breakfast. Please tell your mother it was delicious."

Turning on her heels she spun around, pulling Josh with her, and hurried toward the door. Josh willingly let her lead him away. Max was waiting eagerly at the door. The second his owner walked into view the dog's tail started wagging.

Abby spotted the furry creature instantly, almost running to him. Rubbing the dog's head, scratching his ears, and hugging his neck. It was obvious that Max enjoyed the attention as he rolled over and begged for a belly rub. Abby loved animals especially dogs.

"Does your dog have a name. He's so lovable."

"His name is Max. By the looks of it, he thinks you're okay too." The overgrown furball was so excited about the new person giving him some attention, he jumped up with his tail was wagging so hard it hit Miss Gibbs and knocked her down. Josh was all out laughing now. Abby tried to keep a straight face but began giggling, unable to stop herself.

Josh helped Miss Gibbs to her feet as Max stood looking as if to say, "What's so funny." Soon the threesome was strolling down the boardwalk, ready to tackle the rest of the day.

"I want to thank you for rescuing me back there. Deputy Anderson, I'm sure is a nice enough man, but..." She wasn't sure what to say. How do you politely say that you don't like someone's company?

"You don't have to explain anything to me. I understand. I've known Randy all my life." Abby could see Josh understood. What a truly nice man the sheriff was. She felt ashamed that she had judged him so poorly.

Josh held his arm out, flashing his pearly white teeth, "Shall we get you home? My friends call me Josh." Abby's heart fluttered, this man was both honorable and handsome. Someone she might like to spend time with.

"Please call me Abby." Slightly blushing she had to look away.

Wanting the company of a man was nothing she ever dreamed she would feel. She had learned over the last few years, her step-father and brother had shown her, that God-fearing men did exist and most men were kind and not cruel.

Wesley had stolen everything from her at the age of twelve. Beatings and torturous nights plagued her. She loathed most men! Yet, now a man stood before her that was everything Wesley was not. Part of her wanted to run and hide in fear from Josh, while the other part of her was drawn to him. New feelings were emerging, ones that she wanted to explore. Was is possible there was a man she could like or even fall in love with?

"You don't need to escort me home Sheriff. It's such a beautiful day. I think I would like to take a walk."

"Would you care to join me on my visit to the Franklin's? I can get us a buggy from the blacksmiths and a lunch from the Café. We can be ready to leave in fifteen minutes. I'm the sheriff, and it's my job to show new comers the area. I think it would be considered proper. Don't you think so?"

Considering the idea for a moment, with a bubbly smile, she agreed. True to his word the three of them; Josh, Abby and Max were headed toward the Franklin place around fifteen minutes later.

***

Abby sat happily, smiling, beside the sheriff on the wagon seat. She wasn't wearing her bonnet today. Josh was glad and wished a strong breeze would come up and blow her hair out of its bun, like he seen it on the boardwalk after his fall on the soap.

They visited and chatted throughout the peaceful morning journey. At lunch, Abby gave Max her piece of chicken from the lunch basket that Josh had gotten from the Café. At first, he was slightly mad over it. He had paid good money for their lunch and she went and fed it to the dog. Then Abby spoke, explaining why she had given the dog her food, and it melted his heart.

"I hope you don't mind that I gave Max my chicken? I have access to as much food as I want, but our animals only have what we give them. They rely on us for food and to take care of them. Max is such a good, sweet dog. I've been so spoiled today and I wanted him to have a special day too." Looking up into the sheriff's eyes, she seemed to be looking for understanding.

His insides were twisting into knots, what was happening to him? He had only met this woman yesterday, yet a voice gnawed deep within him, this was the one. Josh had been praying for years for God to show him when, and if, the right woman came along. He didn't think he would ever get married. He felt that working as a law officer, being in life threating situations and away from home a lot, was not the life for a married man. Why he continued to pray about a wife, he wasn't sure.

Was the voice only him being silly, having a crush on a pretty girl? Or was the Lord really speaking to him? He continued to search himself and his emotions for truth. As his eyes gazed into the lovely brown eyes of the petite woman, he knew one thing for a fact. His mind was no longer on a piece of chicken, his deputy, or a lawman's dangerous life. It was on something of far more value, the heart of a woman.

Chapter 5

Not having been chosen, R.J. returned from his missions' interview. Before returning to his house, he stopped by the jail and filled the sheriff in on all of the details. He had admitted to Josh he was relieved that he wasn't selected and explained why.

R.J. told Sheriff Cole that his heart wasn't in faraway places, it was with homeless, needy, and orphaned children. Josh knew that Martha and R.J. had taken children into their home from time to time. With so many families not able to care for their children, the Johnson's felt it was a calling to step in and help.

Josh admired his pastor for it, but was also relieved that R.J. would be staying in Cedar Creek. He wanted to let a real pastor do all of the marrying people. He had not had to officiate a marriage yet but felt nervous just thinking about it.

Later that day, whistling a happy melody, Josh hurried up the narrow and worn path leading to the church. Two weeks had flown by since Abby first came into town on the stage. They had spent almost every day together. Today they were going to Anderson's Café for some of Momma Anderson's famous cinnamon rolls. They were Josh's personal favorite.

Half way up the path, the beautiful, brown eyed girl came bouncing down the trail toward him. The green scarf that she always wore blew in the wind. The sun had only been risen about ten minutes. It cast a brilliant light behind Abby, creating a heavenly glow around her as she approached. Josh's heart skipped a beat. If this woman wasn't an angel, she was as close as anyone could get.

Without a word, no conversation was needed, Josh extended his hand for his sweetheart to take hold. Enjoying the splendor of God's handiwork, the creation of the most vivid sunrise they had ever seen, they began walking in silence.

Abby let loose of Josh's hand at the edge of town. Josh knew that she thought it might appear improper, but he thought that idea was silly. People knew they were seeing each other, and he was proud to show the world that this woman was accompanied by him.

After collecting two large sweet rolls, the happy couple found a seat at one of the tables outside on the boardwalk in front of the café. They were becoming comfortable with each other, sharing stories of their lives. Mostly Josh talked and Abby listened.

She did share a few stories about her birth father, from when she was very young girl. She painted a happy picture about her father through a child's eyes, a hero who loved her.

Josh noticed that part of her childhood, her early teenage years, were missing. She never spoke of them. If he brought it up or asked a question, she quickly changed the subject. He didn't press the matter, figuring that she would tell him when she was ready. He guessed she must have been an awkward teenager and was embarrassed about it.

He wasn't sure why, but sometimes he felt a deep hurt within her and a danger close by. He had been a lawman for four years and he had learned his gut instincts were usually right. In Abby's case, he convinced himself he was being paranoid. Who would want to hurt the sweetest, kindest, most lovable woman in the world?

As he watched her nibble at her roll, he noticed her scarf. She wore it every day. Curiosity was getting to him.

"Abby, can I ask you something?" Josh couldn't stand it any longer. At first, Josh believed she was vain, the scarf was fancy and she wanted to show it off, flaunting her wealth.

Having spent much time with her lately, he had grown to know her character better now. She was not a spoiled rich girl, nor did she wear expensive clothing. She didn't talk about wanting material things either. What she discussed most was the love of her family. Her mother Grace, her father John, and her brother Dakota.

When she talked about them her eyes lit up and excitement filled her voice. It was obvious that she loved them all very much. What Josh most enjoyed hearing about was her love for God, her love of Christ. Everything about this woman was meek and loving. Nothing was vain or puffed up. So why did she always wear that scarf? His curiosity got the best of him.

"Of course, you can." She smiled reassuringly at him but looked a bit uneasy. Josh thought this odd, but who can understand a woman's mind?

"I can't help but notice that you wear this scarf every day." He softly touched it, tracing the edge with his finger. "May I ask why? Not that there's anything wrong with doing so, I'm just wondering."

Immediately her countenance changed. Her head dropped down, her hands went to her lap as she nervously twiddled her thumbs together. Josh didn't understand what he had said that would cause such a reaction, but he patiently waited for her to respond.

"It was six or seven years ago. I was around fourteen. Days and nights all ran together back then. Some of my childhood was not like other girls of my age. Part of it was very rough to say the least, and I don't like to talk about it much." Not making eye contact with Josh, she continued.

"During that time in my Life, I would occasionally help an elderly man with small chores. His name was Zeak Watson. He owned the mercantile store next door to where I lived. One afternoon, while I was in his store, I found a ladies clothing catalog. As I flipped through the pages, I spotted a scarf that I admired. I fell in love with it on sight. I finished browsing in the catalogue and then put it back where I found it."

"Weeks, if not months later, I went into Mr. Watson's store. He handed me a package and said it was my payment for helping him. He must have seen me admire it a dozen times but I had no idea that he had seen me doing it. He secretly ordered it for me."

"This was the first time in my life that I had ever earned anything, and more importantly, it was the first gift that I had ever received. No strings attached, a gift of pure love from his heart. I kept it with me always, I treasure it. I often wonder what became of Mr. Watson. He was a man above most men. I'll always have special place in my heart for him."

Still she kept her head down as she spoke. Josh could see she was uncomfortable and didn't want to talk about it, so he let the matter end. He wondered what had happened in her past to cause such a change in her demeanor. His heart ached for her, but he didn't know why or how to make things better for her.

Gently he took her hand in his. His voice was kind, "Mr. Watson sounds like a good man."

***

The black stallion came to a sudden halt on a hillside beside a small white church. Its rider pulled back hard on the reins. "Steady boy, steady I say!" The rider slapped the dangling reins against his leg, causing a mist of dust to rise. His clothing was caked with dirt from being on the trail far too long. Ignoring the fog of dust, the horse's rider surveyed his surroundings.

He saw a little brook that ran adjacent to the church and flowed downhill straight into a waterwheel at a mill. A few yards to the east of that sat the mercantile store and a café.

The next building, the Cedar Creek Jail, caused a groan to escape from the man's lips. He leaned his head over slightly to the side of the horse and spit on the ground. A few other unmarked buildings, along with three or four small houses. That's all there was. One road and a few buildings.

"Finding someone here should be easy. You're so close to getting what's coming to you! Revenge, at long last, is at my fingertips. Giddy up, get moving!" he yelled at his horse.

He dug his spurs into the innocent animal's side, urging it forward. A smile spread across his entire face, as his evil intentions were spoken.

"It's time to find the teacher. I have a poisonous apple to deliver."

***

As Josh and Abby sat at the outdoor table in front of Anderson's Café, Rebecca watched them from the store window across the street. The couple appeared to be in love, smiling at each other, laughing and chatting. No one needed to hear them say their feeling towards each other, their body language told it all.

At one-point Abby seemed distressed about something. Josh reached across the table and touched her hand, patting it gently. He was undoubtedly in love with the woman.

"Am I ever going to find a husband?" Rebecca spoke out loud to herself. The store was empty, leaving Rebecca completely alone with her thoughts.

"I always assumed it would be me who married Josh. I don't love him and I truly like Abby, so why am I feeling so down today?" Turning her back on the window, she walked to the front counter. Looking at her reflection in the glass case, she asked one more question.

"Father in heaven, I desperately long for a husband. Am I to be married? Is there someone out there for me? Will I ever find a handsome prince charming to whisk me off of my feet like Abby did?"

"Will I do?" A voice echoed from behind her. Startled Rebecca spun around. A well over six-foot-tall man, whom she had never seen before stood before her. His face was mostly hidden by a few weeks or more growth of a beard and long, straight, black hair touched his shoulders. He wore black pants, a white shirt and a black hat. He had a beaming smile making him appear to be a friendly sort of fellow.

"You startled me Sir. How did you get inside without the bell jingling? She asked with heated cheeks.

Taking Rebecca's hand, the stranger placed a kiss on the back of it. "I do apologize Miss. I didn't mean to sneak up on you or frighten you. The little bell did ring when I came inside. You must have been deep in your thoughts of a prince." He grinned flirtatiously and released her hand.

More heat filled the woman's face. "I feel somewhat embarrassed Sir. My apologies, I don't normally go around talking to myself." Changing the subject, she rapidly added, "May I help you find something?"

"Tell me Miss, does this Abby, whom you spoke off really have a prince? I have not had the pleasure of meeting anyone of royalty before."

'Oh, heavens no." Rebecca chuckled out loud. "Though Sheriff Cole might be a prince in her book, he's far from royalty."

"A sheriff. That does change things." The tall man's countenance changed as he whispered his words, looking as if in deep thought. Glancing back toward the store clerk, recovering his cheerful smile, the man continued.

"Are all of the women in this town as pretty as you? If they are, then I believe I will stick around Cedar Creek a while longer than I thought. Besides, I've heard that a handsome prince might be needed?"

With a sparkle in his eye, he boldly grabbed Rebecca's hand. With his free hand he placed it behind her, on her waist. He then gave her a spin away from him, then rapidly spun her back into his arms. Their eyes met, Rebecca's checks turned fiery red as her heart raced.

Slowly he released his grip on her, taking a step back and away. The lady store clerk stood motionless, stunned. The tiny bell on the door gave a jingle as two ladies walked inside. Quickly regaining her composure, Rebecca gave a small wave to the other women.

The man in black spoke loudly, so all could clearly hear him. "I'm new to the area Miss. Are there any lodging accommodations in town?" His eyes held firm on Rebecca, as if all business.

"My mother has a spare room on the side of Anderson's Café. Occasionally she rents it out. I'm sure you would find it acceptable." She gave a faint smile at the stranger.

At that moment, one of the women who had come in called out to her, "Miss Anderson, I forgot my egg basket. I'm going to run home and fetch it. I will be back momentarily." Both ladies hurried out the door, not giving the man in black a second look.

Rebecca's attention was now fully on the mystery man, who stood before her. The man in black also watched the ladies as they hurried away. Turning back to Miss Anderson, he went on with his conversation.

"Thank you, Miss, for the recommendation of a decent place to stay. I've been traveling a long way and have slept many nights on a hard, stony ground. A soft bed would be welcomed."

"I almost forgot to ask." The tall man took a step closer to her. "May I have the pleasure of knowing your name?" Taking Rebecca's hand again in his, he held it, waiting for a response.

"Uh, umm, Becca, I mean Rebecca. Rebecca Anderson," she looked away, obviously embarrassed. Placing a soft kiss on her hand, he took a step closer, his body touched hers.

"It is a pleasure to meet you Miss Anderson." Rebecca's hand began to tremble. Her breathing grew faster.

The man in black's voice was deep as he spoke. "You are a vision of pure loveliness. I intend to get to know you better, much better my dear." With that said he stepped back releasing her hand, turned and walk toward the door.

"Wait," Rebecca called out, "I don't know your name Sir?"

Stopping, he turned, casting an almost devious smile, "Wesley, Ma'am. Wesley Roberts at your service, but you can call me Prince."

Chapter 6

Abby hadn't seen her friend this happy before. Rebecca had excitedly told Abby about meeting a man that had come into the store. She described him as tall, handsome, and charming in a rugged sort of way. Rebecca added that he was unshaven with disheveled and dusty clothing.

She thought the rugged cowboy must have been on his way back from a long cattle drive or perhaps been a rancher because of his appearance. Rebecca liked that idea, telling Abby that she had always wanted to live on a ranch and move away from her father's store.

She said that she loved her parents and appreciated her job, but was ready to lead her own life. One filled with a loving husband, children, and a family of her own.

She had confessed to Abby that her prince caused her cheeks to blush and made her stomach feel strange. Abby knew those feelings, and had experienced them herself. It's the same way she felt each time Josh was near her, it was the feeling of love.

Abby wondered if anyone could be in love after meeting only once? She wasn't sure, but if this mystery man could make Rebecca as happy as Josh made her, then she was all for it. Abby wanted to find out all the details about this new mysterious prince. His real name, how long he was planning to stay in town, and what he looked like. A typical female, Abby thought to herself. The teacher in her wanted a ten-page report, she giggled to herself.

Before Abby had a chance to ask her friend any of her many questions, Rebecca's mother, Mrs. Anderson rushed into the store. She seemed rattled, mumbling something about a letter, her sister's broken ankle, and sending help for a few days.

Rebecca's mother hurriedly took her daughters hand, leading her away, babbling all the way out the door. Abby couldn't recall ever hearing anyone chatter so fast.

Abby agreed with what she heard of the conversation. Helping those in need, especially family, was important. She hoped that she could inquire about the gentleman who had charmed her friend almost off of her feet very soon.

Long after both Anderson women had left, Abby couldn't get her mind off of love, or Sherriff Joshua Cole. She hadn't felt this joyful in her entire life. She felt deep in her heart that she wanted to spend every second, for the rest of her life, with this man. Max too, they were a package deal, and she loved them both.

As her thoughts filled with dreams of love and marriage, a content and peaceful feeling came over her. Nothing could bring her down, her life was absolutely perfect.

***

Wesley gazed out the window of his newly acquired rental room at the back of the Anderson's Café. With a grunt, he turned to look around the meager little room. It wasn't much to look at, nothing like what he was accustomed to back in California. It was small, poorly decorated, and it smelled musky.

It would have to do for now, being the only place available except for the stable, which he had refused immediately when it was offered to him.

Staring at the old broken-down mattress, which was covered with a simple quilt, he sighed. Earlier, he had carelessly tossed his saddle bags onto the bed spilling out some of its contents. Spotting the whip, which had partially fallen out across the bed, he swiftly snatched it up.

With a firm grip and a snap of his wrist, he cracked the long strip of leather against the door post. The tip hit hard, leaving a thin indention in the wood.

"A sheriff, a low-down rotten sheriff. Of all the men in the world that Abby could have taken up with, why did it have to be a sheriff? She's always been a thorn in my side, but not for much longer!"

The whip struck with a popping noise as it hit its mark again, leaving a second, deeper gash beside the first one. Throwing the whip back onto the bed with force, he began to pace. Swiftly he reached into his pant pocket, pulling out a gold pocket watch. Flipping the cover open, he read the time. It was twelve o'clock sharp.

Glancing at himself in the tiny mirror, which hung on the wall above the dresser, he checked his appearance. An obvious bath was in order, but the hunger noises coming from his stomach won the battle of things to do first. Grabbing his hat, he headed out the door.

It only took a few steps to get around the building to the front entrance to the café. A big shaggy gray and black dog lay near the doorway, partially blocking the doorway. As Wesley approached, the animal raised its head and bared his teeth, letting out a low growl.

"Stay out of my way dog, or I'll shoot you, mangy mutt!" Dusting himself off the best that he could, avoiding the dog, he entered the diner. Wesley's eyes roamed the room spotting several tables with people eating.

Something or someone caught his eye. Toward the far end of the cafe, near a window sat two men. One wore a shiny star on his vest, that stood out like the sun in the sky. It was a sheriff's badge.

Casually, Wesley made his way through the room, between several tables and the crowd of people, toward an empty table directly behind the man with the badge.

As he neared, the sheriff looked up, made eye contact, but then continued talking with the other gentleman who was seated at the table with him. Silently, Wesley sat down in the chair directly behind the lawman.

Sheriff Cole noticed a man who he wasn't familiar with, as he approached. Josh had more important things on his mind besides a stranger in town looking for a meal. Normally he made it a point to greet anyone visiting Cedar Creek, but not today. This day, his mind was on something else. Something that made the palms of his hands sweat and his heart race.

"Hello Sir." A young lady with an apron placed a menu in front of Wesley, as she added, "I'll be back shortly to take your order." With a smile, she hurried away to refill a coffee for a gentleman across the room. Picking up the menu, he scanned the food choices. Voices from the table behind him drifted into his ears, making listening to their conversation unavoidable.

"What was your momma all upset about earlier? She was running around like a chicken with its head cut off, mumbling about needed to hurry and helping her sister?" Josh looked puzzled and waited for Randy to answer.

"She received a wire about Aunt Molly, momma's sister. Molly fell and sprained, or possibly broke her ankle. Aunt Molly isn't married or ever had any children. She doesn't have anyone to help her or take care of her.

Momma is worried how she will get around being all alone. So, she decided that she would send Rebecca to stay with Auntie for a few days, to make sure everything is okay. Rebecca didn't want to go, but momma insisted."

"Why not? That's not like Rebecca, not wanting to help others when they need it. Doesn't she like your aunt?"

"She loves her, we all do. Aunt Molly is a hoot. She is a joyous, fun person to be around, always telling stories, jokes, and making our time with her enjoyable. If I tell you the real reason Rebecca doesn't want to go, you can't breathe a word to anyone."

"Now you have my curiosity up. I won't say a word, spill it. Tell me already."

"Well," Randy paused, making Josh even more impatient. "She met a man and is smitten with him, to say the least. I've never seen her this way. She's been walking around with her head in the clouds and a big smile. She acts in love if you ask me, and she just met this man. Crazy huh?" Randy chuckled.

Josh smiled, "Not as crazy as you think. Look how fast I fell for Abby. Speaking of Abby, I need to talk to you about something."

As both men talked, Abby's name got Wesley's full attention. The waitress had come and gone, taking his order, now he sat waiting on his meal with nothing to do but listen.

"Ok, I'm all ears, you have my full attention." The deputy looked at the sheriff, "What about Abby?"

"It's no secret that I'm in love with her. Randy, I can't keep her out of my mind, I dream of her even. There is only one thing that I can do, I've decided to ask her to marry me. I want you to be my best man." Josh's smile beamed as he waited to see his friend's response.

"Married? I don't know whether to have you checked out by the doctor because you're delirious or congratulate you." Randy laughed loudly.

"I'm kidding, ole buddy, I am very happy for you. Abby is a truly a nice person and will make a fine wife." He reached across the table and shook the groom's hand.

"When do you think your going to pop the question?" Randy asked. "Do I still have time to steal her away from you?" he laughed. "Just kidding you around."

"I haven't thought that far ahead yet. One thing for sure though, this one's not getting away. I'd do anything for her. Between me and you Randy, sometimes when I look into her eye's I see something there."

"What do you mean, what kind of something?"

"I don't know how to explain it, but its almost like a deep hurt or fear. She has never expressed anything other than happiness in her life. I can tell you one thing, I think if anyone ever tried to hurt her, I'd defend her with my own life."

A deep protectiveness arose in him. A strong sense that Abby's life was in imminent danger was so over powering that Josh unconsciously placed his hand on his gun.

Pulling some money from his pocket, Wesley tossed it on the table. Wiping his mouth with a cloth napkin, he placed it on the table. Standing, scooting his chair back under the table, he headed for the exit.

Getting past the overgrown furball wasn't easy, but Wesley was quick on his feet. He was out and down the boardwalk before the dog noticed. That didn't stop the animal from growling. Wesley laughed and called back to the dog, as if it could understand him.

"Ha, ha mutt. Ole Wesley's too fast for you. Maybe next time? Nah, probably not." He laughed as he hurried away.

He opened the door of his room and hurried inside, slamming the door shut behind him. Rushing to fetch the water basin that hung on the wall, it was almost two o'clock. He had run into Mrs. Anderson right after leaving the café.

She explained to him that she had arranged for hot water for a bath to be brought to his room at two o'clock sharp. He didn't have time to spare, the water would be there any minute.

Catching sight of his refection in the mirror, he ran his fingers though his beard. He eyed his appearance. His clothes were wrinkled and dirty. Raising his arm to his nose, he sniffed the sleeve of his shirt. Wrinkling his nose, it was time for a shave and bath.

A grin lit his face, "My dear Abby, your precious sheriff Cole is going to get a visitor soon, and so are you." The grin left his face, as he clinched his fists tightly.

He added, "I've waited years for this. I'll have my revenge before this week is over. I'm going to take everything that's dear to you just like you did me, including your sheriff. I'm going to rip your heart out with great satisfaction."

Wesley stepped forward, his face almost touching the looking glass. He hissed his words like a serpent. "With evil desires and wicked intentions. I'm coming for you!

Chapter 7

The gentle rain sounded peaceful as it slowly lulled Abby toward sleep. Her eyes fluttered closed, then open again, landing on the green scarf which lay on her dresser. Memories of Zeak flashed into her mind. Soon she fell into a deep sleep and began to dream.

Curled up tightly, Abby lay on her bed at the Roberts Saloon. Every noise, footstep, or creak in the building startled her, sending fear and panic through her veins. She wondered if the nightly visits would ever stop? Please, she dared to hope, let them stop!

It had been a torturous year since the monster, as she called him, Wesley Roberts took her in when her father died. She often wondered why the only person in the world who loved her had to be shot and killed? Why had fate been so cruel to her? The men at the poker game had wanted his money, and they got it. How it pained her, knowing that she would never see her father again.

Her thoughts swiftly turned fearful, it would be dark outside soon. She dreaded the night and hated what came with it. Every sound caused her to jump. She thought briefly about running away again, but she knew Wesley would find her, he always did, and then he would inflict a punishment.

Wesley enjoyed using his belt, or a leather whip, for the majority of her "lessons", as he called them. She didn't want another beating or broken bone. Running away was not an option anymore. She saw no way out alive, but was living this life any better?

Zeak Watson, the mercantile owner next door, had tried to help her escape a couple of times. Wesley's hired men ransacked the store and roughed up the older gentleman pretty bad. Abby wasn't sure how old Zeak was, but he looked one hundred and not strong enough to defend himself against so many young men.

Not wanting anyone else to suffer because of her, she had no choice but to endure Wesley's lessons. Her existence was misery and torture. She hated herself and her life, but most of all, she loathed Wesley Roberts. Without any remorse, she wished him dead.

She had worked hard today, her body told her so, every muscle ached. Wesley ordered her to wash and change all the bedding in each room of the saloon, starting with his. She scrubbed all of the floors in the entire building. Then she swept the porch and carried fresh water to all the basins in each bed chamber. Lastly, she carried wood into the kitchen and filled the wood box.

It had taken from sun up to almost sundown, but it was done. Abby was beyond exhausted, not able to force her eyes to remain open any longer, slowly they began to close.

BAM... The door made a loud, thunderous noise as it bounced against the wall. Abby jumped as her eyes shot open to see a large form filling her doorway. She knew who it was and what he wanted. Instantly she began to cry, feeling sick to her stomach.

"Why are you asleep this early? You're lazy and almost worthless." Wesley slurred his words, clearly intoxicated. "Why do I tolerate your

laziness? I should toss you to the miners. You're almost of no use to me at all, almost..." *A grin lit his face as he moved into her room.*

***

"NOOO…" Abby suddenly woke with a scream. Slightly disoriented, breathing heavily, her heart raced. She had broken out in a cold sweat. Realizing that it was only a terrible dream, she tried to calm down. She had not seen or heard from Wesley in over five years. He didn't know where she was, and she hoped that he never would.

The rain had stopped, letting soft moonlight shine through the window, landing on her dresser. As her eyes adjusted to dim light, something didn't feel right. An uneasiness hovered in the room, as if the presence of evil was nearby. Slowly she scanned the darkened room. Shadows danced in every corner.

She was convinced that her mind must be playing tricks on her, there was nothing to be afraid of. As the battle in her mind weaved back and forth, the dresser caught her eye. Something was different. That's when she noticed that her beloved scarf was missing. Was she seeing things? Wasn't it there a moment ago? Rubbing her eyes, she looked again, still no scarf.

She rose from her bed for a closer look. It must have fallen onto the floor. It wasn't fancy but it gave her a sense of comfort and peace, like a child and their security blanket. She began looking around, as much as the low lighting would allow. No luck, where could it have gone? Maybe a breeze blew it the under something.

"Are you looking for something?" A familiar voice whispered from the darkest part of the room, directly behind her.

Abby froze, her heart began to pound. Did she imagine it, had she lost her mind completely? Her hands started to tremble and her knees felt weak, slowly she forced herself to turn around.

A match strike was heard as light illuminating the shadows, revealing her worst fear. Wesley lit a small candle in his hand. He spoke with a deep low voice.

"It's been a long time my dear." Abby saw that he held her cherished scarf in his hand. "Why do you still have this old thing?" Looking her straight in the eye, without flinching, he began to tear the green material easily into shreds. Abby knew he expected her to cry, as he carelessly tossed the pieces on the floor with a smirk.

She watched helplessly as her treasure was destroyed and lay on floor like trash to him. The scarf was valuable to her but not as much as her life. Her safety was her main concern.

She stole a quick glance toward her door leading outside. It was bolted shut, it would take too long to open it, Wesley was only a few feet away and could stop her easily. Trying not to be obvious she looked to the door leading into the church.

"Don't try to escape Abby. You know what I will do to you if you run from me." His voice was cold. She remembered him being violent but his voice told her he was past that. He was deadly. Her only hope was to show no fear. She silently prayed for the Lord to give her strength and courage.

"Get out of my room. I demand that you get out this instant." She couldn't conceal the quiver in her voice.

"Is that any way to greet me after all this time?" Eyeing her up and down, "You've grown into a fine-looking woman. I have a much better idea of how I should be welcomed." With a grin he let out a whistle.

"Get out!" Knowing she was trapped, her only hope was to bluff him. "I don't' know how you found me but you are not welcome here. Get out now!" She held his gaze trying to look as fierce as possible.

The smirk on his face faded. A tight jaw with clenched teeth took its place. "You don't get to tell me what to do or order me anywhere! We have unfinished business. In case your little pea brain has forgotten, you robbed me. I'm here to collect."

"You are going to give me back every cent you took, with interest." His hands reached for the whip that was clipped to his side like a gun. Swiftly untying it, he pulled the long piece of brown leather out with a snap. Stepping forward he glared at Abby with furrowed brows.

"I've waited so long for this; my revenge will be sweet." Before Abby had a chance to react, Wesley rushed forward, tightly grasping her arm. Quickly spinning her around, he hurled her onto the bed. She landed on her stomach with a grunt, without any time to regain her composure, she felt the first strike of the whip.

A scream escaped her lips. Wesley had lashed her many times over the years. She thought she would have toughened up, but each time hurt as bad as the last. A single tear trickled down her cheek as dozens of horrid memories flooded into her mind. Please God, help me!

Without warning she felt his large hands hit her back, tearing her nightgown open, exposing her skin.

"You are going to wish you were dead by the time I'm done with you. No one double crosses Wesley Roberts, especially a good for nothing female." He lifted his hand high above his head, ready to strike hard, with a vengeance.

***

After tossing and turning for several hours, Josh finally decided to crawl out of his bed in the back room of the Cedar Creek jail. It didn't take him long to get a pot of coffee brewing. While he waited on it to heat, a brown eyed beauty filled his thoughts, the reason sleep eluded him.

Today was the big day. In only a few more hours he was going to travel to Forsyth, to the jewelry store, a fella needs a ring to propose. His mind was made up, he would ask Abby to marry him this Saturday. He had it all planned out. They would meet at Momma Anderson's for dinner. He would get down on one knee and confess his intentions.

As excited as he was, Josh had a few reservations about leaving for an entire day. Putting his deputy in charge for that long, worried him. He worried if Randy could handle it if there was an emergency or wave of criminal activity that broke out. He tried to convince himself those things were unlikely to happen, besides his dog would be there to help. There wasn't a more loyal companion in the world, Max would have Randy's back.

Some people didn't think that animals could understand people, Josh knew better. His dog could sense danger, sniff out any bad guy, and was an excellent judge of character. If Max didn't like a person, Josh was leery of them as well. Over and over, that shaggy gray dog had proved himself to be right. Yes, Max could keep watch over Randy.

Josh poured his first cup of coffee for the day. Blowing on it, to help cool it down faster, he stepped outside on the boardwalk in front of the jail. He sat down on a rough plank bench, his usual spot to watch the sunrise. As the steam rose from the hot liquid, it reminded him of a foggy morning when all the earth seemed peaceful and still. Those were some of his favorite times.

Josh loved the outdoors and planned one day to have a home with a porch across the entire front of it. He wouldn't miss a sunrise or sunset ever if he had his way. After he and Abby were married, they could sit outside together each day. He could whittle wooden animals while she knitted a sweater or sewed his socks. It sounded like the perfect life, one he was ready to begin.

His mind roamed to other parts of their future home. It would have large windows, Abby had mentioned how much she liked to see the curtains blow in the breeze on a summer day. He wanted every detail of the design to please his new bride, but first thing first. He hadn't even asked her yet.

Reaching into his vest pocket, pulling out his watch, he checked the time. It was only five a.m. His heart quickened, only a few more hours and he would be on his way to purchase the ring.

It was biscuit and gravy day, the special at the Café each Thursday morning. He had made plans to meet Abby there at seven thirty. He planned tell her that he was going out of town on a business trip for a day or two.

As the first light of dawn began to peek out over the horizon, Josh began to let his mind clear and let out a yawn.

"Now that it's time to get up, I'm tired?" Josh chuckled to himself. Grasping his cup, he quickly headed back inside to refill his coffee, sleep would not overtake him.

***

"Hold it right there, Mister! Don't you strike that girl one more time." Reverend Johnson rushed into the room, placing his body between the man holding the whip and Abby.

In the of a blink of an eye, Wesley had his revolver drawn and pointed at the intruder. "I don't know who you are or what you're doing here, but I'm warning you to get out of my way. This isn't any of your business. You better get out now if you know what's good for you." Wesley pulled his gun, cocking the trigger and moving the barrel's tip close to the chest of the other man.

"I'm Reverend Anthony Johnson, and this is my church. Everything that goes on in this building is my business. I'm not a five foot, one-hundred-pound girl. I am a six foot four, well over two-hundred-pound grown man."

"I've worked hard all of my life, and I'm not soft. There's a lot of strength in this body yet. I know my creator and I'm not afraid to die. Can you say the same?" R.J. held his ground without flinching or backing down.

"You don't have a gun, but I do, and it's aimed at your heart. If I pull this trigger, I can drop you dead in seconds. I'd say I have the advantage. I'll give you one last chance to get out of here. If you don't, I'm going to kill you without a second thought," With a smirk he added, "Then you can meet that creator of yours."

While the two men faced off, Abby grabbed the robe that was tossed over her headboard and put it on. She quickly scurried to the furthest corner of the room. She watched as a Godly man stood toe to toe with pure evil.

"If you kill a man of God, every lawman in the country will be hunting you. Your face will be on wanted posters everywhere. You will spend the rest of your life looking over your shoulder."

"And, in case you don't know it, the sheriff of this town is sweet on this woman. If you hurt her in any way, Sheriff Cole will track you to the ends of the earth. It's your choice." R.J. held the strangers gaze, his shoulders squared, ready for anything. Abby could tell he would do whatever it took to help her.

As scared as she was, the Reverend defending her and his words touched her heart. She prayed for his safety, and hers. Time seemed to be in slow motion. Observing Wesley's face, she could clearly read his emotions. He was weighing all the things the Reverend had spoken. Suddenly, with a grunt, Wesley holstered his gun.

Looking to Abby he gruffly spoke, "You may have gotten away this time, but I will be back. Next time you won't have a bodyguard to protect you."

Looking back to R.J. he gruffly spoke. "You have given me a challenge. I will find a way around the law and your God if need be. Until then, stay out of my way preacher man."

Turning, Wesley stomped out the door, slamming it so hard the window rattled. The man in black stormed away and out of sight. R.J. hurried to the door, closing and bolting it securely.

He looked at Abby, "Are you ok Miss Gibbs, do you want me to fetch Martha to help you in any way?" His face shown genuine concern.

Shaking her head, no, Abby remained huddled in the corner, still somewhat in shock. Slowly she stood, holding her robe tightly closed. Taking the few steps toward the bed she sat down, her legs felt weak and her mind raced. How had Wesley found her? What was she going to do now?

She couldn't stay in Cedar Creek, she had to leave immediately.

"Miss Gibbs, I think we need to talk." R.J. spoke in a gentle caring tone. "Splash some water on your face, get dressed, and then come out in the sanctuary. I will be waiting. Take all the time you need." With that said, he left the room, pulling her door closed tightly behind him.

Abby never thought this day would come. She certainly didn't want anyone to find out about her past. It was humiliating to her, she didn't want to tell anyone, especially a pastor.

Shame overwhelmed her, followed by panic. Wesley would be lurking nearby. It wasn't safe for her any longer. She knew she owed R.J. an explanation.

He would have to find a replacement teacher as well. There was so much to do. She would have to be packed and ready to leave on the next stage, which was due to come in tomorrow, Friday. In the short time she'd lived in Cedar Creek, she had grown fond of so many people. She even loved one, Josh, deeply.

She had found her soulmate, her true love. What would she tell Josh? Her heart ached and she began to sob. How could she leave him? Of all the punishments and pain Wesley had put her through over the years, none compared to the pain of leaving Josh. As she wept, the front of her robe became saturated with tears.

After the tears slowed, she did as R.J. had instructed her, splashed cold water on her face and got dressed. Taking a deep breath, she entered the church sanctuary. Feeling lost, hopeless, and ashamed beyond compare, she met R.J.'s gaze.

He was sitting on the front pew, smiling kindly at her, probably to reassure her everything would be alright. Abby felt like nothing could ever be okay again.

"I locked the doors in the front of the church as well, you're completely safe. I will stay here to make sure he doesn't bother you again tonight. I'm going to jump right to the point. Who was he and why does he want to hurt you?" He waited patiently for Abby to speak.

"It all began when I was around twelve years old. My father went into a saloon and brothel, that was owned by Wesley Roberts, the man who was just here, looking for a poker game. My mother had passed away years ago, I had no other relatives. My father was my whole life, where he went, I went. That night he was shot and killed, leaving me devasted and all alone in this world. Wesley decided to take me in." Abby looked down, she was so embarrassed to go on, but knew she must.

"In the beginning, I was forced to cook and clean, but soon he began visiting my room at night." She looked up into the Reverend's eyes. Tears were now rolling down her face.

R.J.'s eyes grew glossy, "I am so sorry. You were only a child." Abby thought she saw tears in his eyes, she had to look away.

Abby continued, "I was beat often, received broken bones, and ran away a few times. He always found me. I felt hopeless, hated my life, and wished Wesley Roberts was dead.

Then one day a man named Dakota Russell rescued me, that's another story though. When he brought me to his home, his mother and step father, John Gibbs adopted me. My real name is Abby Mathews. I have only been Abby Gibbs for the last five years."

Over the next hour Abby filled R.J. in on her past with detail. At first, she was reluctant to share so much, but as she talked to the man of God, she felt relieved.

After they spoke, R.J. agreed that she wasn't safe alone any longer. He insisted she stay with Martha and himself until she could get on the Friday stage. Abby considered it briefly, but thought it was for only one more night and she didn't want to put the Johnson's in any danger.

As dawn approached, though still concerned for Abby's safety, Abby convinced R.J. to check on Martha. He reassured her that he would be back shortly, to walk her into town to meet Josh. Abby promised that she would keep the door locked.

Before he left, Abby asked, almost begged the Reverend not tell a soul her secret, especially Josh. R.J. reluctantly agreed.

"I will be back soon. Keep those doors locked. If an emergency arises, ring the church bells. It will be our signal that something is wrong. And Abby…?"

Looking up into his caring eyes, "Yes?" Abby answered.

"You are a brave woman, who has walked through a hell on this earth. I don't believe God would pull you from the sea to let you drown in the river. Keep your faith and know that if God is for you, then who can be against you?" With that said, he left.

All alone, silence rang out in her ears. How could silence be so loud? She felt fear start to rise up, as if it was trying to devour her. She wouldn't go back to a life with Wesley, she wouldn't! Her legs felt stiff, her body paralyzed.

"Lord help me. I've not been this afraid before. I can't go back." She began to weep. She didn't know what to do? "Lord forgive what I'm about to say, but I'd rather die first."

Chapter 8

The whip struck against the door post for the third time, leaving gashes marred into the wood. Wesley spun around, letting the long piece of leather hit at random anything in its path. He paced back and forth in the small room, like a caged animal.

"She will not get away with this. I will find a way to punish her severely." Hurling the whip across the room, Wesley let out a loud growl and thrust his fist into the wall. "Ouch..." Clutching his hand in pain, he inspected the injured area. His knuckles were scraped and bleeding, working his fingers open and closed, nothing seemed to be broken.

"Calm down, before you really hurt yourself. Think man, think. There must be a way around the law. A way to take Abby out of this rotten town freely." Deep in thought, he began to pace again. Catching sight of his refection in the mirror, he paused to look at himself. He pushed a piece of hair away from his face.

"Don't let her get to you Wesley. You're a man, far more superior than any woman could ever hope to be. If anyone can find a way to avoid the law, it's you!"

He walked around a few minutes longer, abruptly stopping, with a smile on his face. A soft chuckle erupted from his throat that swiftly turned to laughter.

"What an ingenious idea! You're brilliant Wesley, 'ole boy, simply brilliant!" Going back to the mirror, he carefully tucked in his shirt, dusted off his pants, and combed his hair. Collecting his hat, he headed out the door.

"Ready or not teacher, here I come!"

***

The aroma of fresh biscuits filled the air at Momma Anderson's. Josh could almost taste the flaky delights, smothered in white gravy. Today he decided to add bacon to his order. Bacon was a food that he couldn't seem to get enough of, on sandwiches, sprinkled on top of a salad, in omelets, and sometimes he would add chopped pieces to his fried potatoes.

As food danced around in Josh's head, he noticed Abby approaching the Café with R.J. at her side. The expressions on both of their faces told Josh that something was amiss. He jumped up and headed to the door to greet them.

"What's wrong Abby? R.J.?" He asked as soon as they stepped through the door.

R.J. spoke, but seemed to avoid Josh's question. "Good morning Sheriff, it's a beautiful day already this morning. I think it's going to be a scorcher today." He flashed a weak smile.

"I hate to say hello and then have to rush away, but Martha has a list of "honey do" jobs a mile long waiting for me." With a wave of his hand, the Reverend left before anyone could reply. Josh looked at Abby with confusion written on his face, clearly wanting to know what was going on.

Abby watched R.J. disappear down the road and around the corner. She didn't seem to want to make eye contact with Josh. It wasn't like her, he knew something was amiss. Both of them were acting strange and were avoiding his questions. He wouldn't give up so easily, he would get to the bottom of it. He was, after all, the sheriff.

"Abby, tell me. What's going on?" His voice was filled with concern but carried an aura of authority.

"Nothing. I'm sorry, I didn't sleep well last night and I'm very tired. R.J. was only keeping me company as I walked here for breakfast. Other than that, there isn't anything to tell." She frowned vaguely at Josh.

He studied her face and body language for a few moments. Was she only tired? She seemed distracted and nervous. He noticed that she wasn't wearing her scarf. Every day she had it on her person, around her neck, waist, or occasionally tied up in her hair. He found it odd it was missing today.

"Where's your scarf Abby?" Josh couldn't help himself, he wanted to know.

Abby wasn't acting like herself. She was still unable to make eye contact with him. She placed her hand to her neck, "Oh, um, I forgot it I guess."

Maybe he was reading more into it than there was? She did have dark circles under her eyes, as if she hadn't slept a wink, poor girl. To have forgotten her beloved scarf, she has to be sleep deprived.

After careful consideration, he convinced himself that it was probably fatigue. Taking her arm, he escorted her to a table in the back corner of the room, seating her by the window. He took the seat beside her.

"I've already ordered biscuits, gravy, bacon, and eggs for both of us. Unless you would prefer something else? I can call the waitress over and add anything you want?" Looking at her downcast face, he added, "Do you need a cup of coffee? Maybe that will help wake you?"

"You're sweet for asking. Have I told you lately what a wonderful man you are and how much you mean to me?" She looked into his eyes. "I have something I need to talk to you about."

Josh couldn't stand it any longer. As he gazed at her lovely face, he knew he loved her with all of his heart and wanted her to know it. "Abby, darling. Have I told you how much I...?"

"Sheriff Cole, Sheriff Cole, come quick!" Randy came rushing to their table, yelling and waving his arms about. "There's a fire at the stable. The horses are spooked and going crazy. Several men are trying to get the animals out before the entire building goes up in flames."

Randy swiftly took a breath and continued, "John Wilson, Tom Banks and few others have formed a water line, but we need more buckets. We need to get this under control before it catches any other buildings on fire or burns down the entire town."

Looking out the window Josh could see black smoke rolling high into the air. There was no time to waste, he jumped up and started to rush away.

Josh looked over his shoulder as he called back to Abby. "I'm sorry. I have to go." In a split second, he was out the door and sprinting down the boardwalk toward the stable.

***

Abby peered out of the window, looking for signs of a fire, easily finding a pillar of smoke rising high into the air. She wondered how she had not noticed that earlier. She should be more aware of her surroundings, especially with Wesley prowling around, he could be anywhere. He surely wouldn't try anything with other people nearby? She swiftly scanned the café.

A couple sat two tables over, happily enjoying their meal. An elderly gentleman was seated at the counter, casually sipping on a cup of coffee. The café was usually completely full, but not today.

She guessed everyone else must be out fighting the fire or being a spectator. She peered out the window, watching as various people of all ages scurried about. She said a silent prayer for the safety of everyone involved, including the animals.

Once breakfast was over, she debated what to do next. Did she dare go back to her room or should she stay in town? She couldn't sit at this table all day, could she? Josh was gone, along with her protection. Placing a hand to her neck, she felt for her scarf which gave her comfort, but it was gone. Saddened, she knew she would never wear it again.

Wesley had torn it to shreds out of pure meanness. She told herself that she didn't need a piece of material to feel safe, and Zeak would always be in her heart. Wesley couldn't take that away from her.

What should she do for the remainder of the day? Reaching into her dress pocket, she pulled out a small, very worn, black, leather Bible. She would read awhile to pass the time, she obviously wasn't leaving the safety of the café.

Abby often read in the mornings. She liked starting her day in God's word. Holding the Bible in her hand, she took notice of its size. She had always wanted a bigger one, but not today. She felt blessed to have one that fit in her pocket. Abby was amazed at all ways that God found to bless her. Even with a tiny Bible.

After reading, she thought about visiting Anderson's Mercantile. It would be a good place to pass the time. She could browse the fabrics, patterns, dry goods, as well as inquire about Rebecca. She dearly missed her friend.

Immediately, sadness struck her. She realized she would never get to see Rebecca, again or say goodbye. Thoughts of Josh, Rebecca and Wesley filled her mind. Tears formed in her eyes. Refusing to cry, she took a deep breath and decided to think on other things. What would she do after her visit to the mercantile?

In the afternoon she could stop by the jail with a picnic lunch for Josh. She hoped the fire would be under control by then, she prayed again for everyone's safety.

Abby wanted to see Max too. She never dreamed that any man and his dog could capture her heart. Josh is as opposite of Wesley as night is from day, or as good is from evil.

"Thank you, Lord, for letting me find a good man. One with a heart that seeks after you. And Lord, I don't know how to handle Wesley being here. Please help me and keep me safe. Amen." Abby felt remorseful. She hadn't been praying like she should, but she knew God was faithful and forgiving.

The waitress appeared, interrupting Abby's thoughts. She held two large plates of food, "Excuse me ma'am, I saw the sheriff run out earlier, I'm guessing to help with the fire? What should I do with Sheriff Cole's breakfast?"

Abby hesitated, she wasn't entirely sure. After a moment to think about it, she decided that it was best to leave it with her. Josh might come back starved. The waitress did as she was instructed and left both plates. Unfortunately, Abby found that she didn't have much of an appetite.

Reaching for the Bible that was on the table, she began to read. Scripture had a way of comforting her. She hoped it would do the same today because she had a very uneasy feeling. She opened it to Psalm 23:1-6 and began reading in a quiet voice.

"The LORD is my shepherd; I shall not want. He makes me to lie down in green pastures; He leads me beside the still waters. He restores my soul; He leads me in the paths of righteousness for His name's sake."

"Yea, though I walk through the valley of the shadow of death, I will fear no evil; For You are with me. Your rod and Your staff, they comfort me. You prepare a table before me in the presence of my enemies; You anoint my head with oil; My cup runs over. Surely goodness and mercy shall follow me all the days of my life; And I will dwell in the house of the LORD Forever."

Before she had a chance to read any more something bumped into her. Someone had sat down next to her. Josh must have returned. Abby's head shot up with a smile and relief filled her heart. What she saw sent cold chills down her spine.

"Hello, I see you ordered me breakfast. How thoughtful, I'm famished." Picking up the napkin and placing it in his lap, Wesley began to devour Josh's breakfast.

Chapter 9

Black haze filled the air, as men carried buckets of water from the mill to the stables. Many town residents scurried about, trying to do what they could to help quench the flames. As each pail of water was tossed onto the burning hay and wood, it caused additional thick smoke to roll, making it hard to see and breathe.

"We need more water and fast." Josh called out to Randy, "Lets run up to your dad's store and collect a few blankets and see if there are any extra buckets. We can wet the blankets and slap out any fire that might try to spread the nearby grassland." Josh wanted to be prepared, there was no time to lose.

As both men ran past the café, they caught sight of Abby. She was still sitting in the same spot at the window, but a man was sitting next to her. Josh didn't recognize the man, apparently Randy didn't either.

"Did you see that guy sitting beside Miss Gibbs? I don't know him, do you?" Randy questioned.

"I may have seen him in town a time or two. Don't you think he was sitting entirely too close to Abby? I didn't like that." Josh was embarrassed that he had voiced his jealousy to Randy.

"Did Abby appear uneasy to you? Her head was down and her hands were in her lap. She tends to do that when she's nervous." Josh a felt stirring in his spirit, like the presence of evil had descended upon Cedar Creek.

Randy shrugged but didn't reply. Josh figured he didn't know how to reply. Randy didn't know Abby like he did. As they reached the Mercantile, Josh tried to keep his mind on the mission at hand, and off of some other man so close to Abby.

As the two lawmen collected the articles they had come for, Josh couldn't stop his thoughts from going wild. That stranger was eating breakfast beside his girl, and she was letting him. If that fire wasn't an emergency, he would march straight into the cafe and physically remove that brash man.

How dare he impose on my almost fiancé? As they rushed back toward the fire, Josh fought the urge to look inside at the stranger and Abby, he knew better. The town needed his complete attention.

He quickly scolded himself for being jealous. Josh knew those kinds of feelings would lead to nothing but trouble. Besides, that gentleman could be her brother, a close friend, or relative who came for a visit. Josh trusted Abby, he was sure that there was a logical explanation.

***

Abby was stunned when Wesley sat down beside her in broad daylight. He wouldn't dare drag her out kicking and screaming, which she would do. She would fight him with every inch of her being. There was no way she would let him take her away without a fight.

She was surprised that her first instinct was to fight instead of being fearful. That's when she realized for the first time in her life, she had a reason to fight, Josh, the man she loved. Never in her wildest dreams did she believe it possible to love a man.

Feeling courageous she spoke, "What are you doing here?" Wesley fed off of weakness and fear. Her voice didn't sound as brave as she felt, as it crackled a little, she cleared her throat. She mustn't let him get mental control over her.

She was in a public place and a grown woman, not a little girl anymore. She had family, friends and God on her side now. Wesley could no longer bully her.

Wesley replied smoothly, "Is that any way to speak to an old, dear friend? I noticed you were sitting here alone. What kind of gentleman would I be if I didn't come to your aide? No lady should be left unaccompanied these days. You never know what kind of predator might be lurking nearby."

Glancing at Abby with a half-sided grin he added, "Besides, we have unfinished business darling." He stuffed the last bite of egg into his mouth, wiped his face with the napkin, then tossed it on the table. Slowly he lifted the coffee cup, drinking the last few gulps in it as well.

"I want you to leave. The meal you ate belonged to the sheriff of this town. He is due back at any moment. He won't take kindly to you sitting in his seat, eating his meal, or trying to harass his girl. You should leave while you still have the chance." Her voice sounded a bit stronger this time, but she knew Josh wasn't coming back anytime soon.

"Shame, shame, shame. You're telling ole Wesley a lie. That sheriff of yours isn't coming back, he's fighting a nasty fire. I sure hope no one get hurts." His facial expression told Abby that he knew something about it.

"What did you do? Did you start that fire?" She already knew the answer. "Don't you care about human lives or about the innocent animals that are trapped in their stalls?" Anger overtook all fear. "You make me sick. You are evil, pure evil. May God have mercy on your soul Wesley Roberts."

Using her shoulder, she nudged Wesley's side, trying to push him out of her way. "Let me out of here. Move out of my way."

"You're not going anywhere. Stop pushing me, hold still, and shut up." Clearly losing his temper, Wesley continued with a harsh tone.

"No more Mr. Nice Guy. I want my money, with interest, and I want it now. I'm sure you don't have one bit of it left after all these years?" He looked to Abby for a response.

She didn't have one. He was right she didn't have it anymore. She had anonymously donated every dollar years ago to a church building fund. She felt that it was ill gotten gains, and it needed to be put to good use.

"Your repayment begins now. Here's what's going to happen. I have a new, brothel in California but I don't have enough girls to go around. You're coming back with me and going to work."

Wesley reached his hand under the table, placing it on Abby thigh. "I have a few installments to collect myself."

Abby quickly snatched his hand, flinging it off her leg. "I will not be one of you girls and I certainly will never do what you're implying!"

She started to push the table forward, she aimed to get away from him, even if she had to crawl under the table to do it. She would run outside and call out for Josh, he would save her, except she needed to get out of this corner first.

Wesley grabbed her wrist tightly. "Hold still and stop creating a scene. If you don't stop it right now, Rebecca will pay for your mistakes."

Instantly she stopped squirming. "What do you mean by that? What does Rebecca have to do with us or any money that I owe you?"

"Rebecca wants to get married, have a family and live happily ever after. So much so, in fact, that she is willing to believe she's in love with a man after meeting him twice. Sounds desperate wouldn't you say?"

"Women like that could be lured away by offers of living in a fine home with servants, wearing eloquent clothing, and enjoying expensive food. And best of all, the love and adoration of a loving handsome husband, such as myself. At least that's what she'd believe would happen. But you and I both know what she would really receive, don't we?"

Wesley dusted a crumb off of his shirt casually. "I have all those things to offer, but Rebecca is not worthy of them, no woman is. I've earned them, me alone, not some country bumpkin looking to get rich off a hard-working businessman like myself."

"Once I have her under my care, we both know there is no escape. She will be put to work the day she arrives. I will work her day and night until she is all used up, then I will toss her out in the street."

Abby's eyes widened. "Rebecca's mystery man, her prince, is you?" She knew Wesley could be charming and that many women swooned over him. She thought him detestable and refused to let her sweet friend be one of those unfortunate souls.

"I won't let that happen to her. I will tell her everything about you, the things you've done to me. How cruel and wicked you really are. She'll never leave with you, once she knows the truth." Abby was sure of it, no person in their right mind would want to be near a man like him.

He grinned, as if unscathed by her remarks. "I'm a prince in her eyes. I might go so far as to say, she might not believe anything you tell her about me. It really doesn't matter though, I'm going to win this battle, missy. And do you know how?" He paused briefly but didn't give her the opportunity to answer. "Because of your ridiculous sense of honor and decency."

Abby, angered by his words, wanted to wipe the smug look off his face. Women did find him handsome, but his attractiveness was external, his insides were rotten and ugly to the bone. Abby knew the real monster inside of him, and found him revolting.

"I won't let her be fooled by you. I will tell her about the sick, cruel monster that lurks inside of you." She didn't care what type of punishment he might try to inflict on her, Rebecca must be warned.

Wesley remained calm, still smiling, so arrogantly sure of himself. "Think back to all those years you lived in my home, under my care? Do you remember the trophies that adorned my bed chamber dresser?" As he spoke, she felt sick, knowing exactly what he was implying.

"Yes," she hung her head. "First place trophy's for sharp shooting. Please don't shoot Rebecca." Abby knew her friend was out of town, but for how long? She shuddered to think, what if her friend was on her way home at this very moment. There wouldn't be any way to protect her or warn her. Abby struggled to fight back the fear that was building inside of her.

"Shoot her? Why do females always need things spelled out for them? You're a real dim whit. Why would I harm such a pretty little money maker? I can guarantee you her safety. On the other hand, I see you're fond of a certain sheriff and his filthy dog. It would be a terrible shame if that mutt was killed."

He looked her in the eyes sending a deadly warning, "Or worse, if the sheriff rode out of town one day and never returned."
Abby knew Wesley always made good on his threats. He meant every word he spoke.

"Are you saying that you're going to kill Josh and Max. Then pretend you want to marry Rebecca, but prostitute her out instead?" Abby felt as if her breath had been knocked out of her. Why did she even ask, she knew the answer?

"That's exactly what I'm saying. Because of my generous nature, I am willing to offer you a deal. If you're a good girl, leave willingly with me, I might spare the others' lives." Wesley reached his hand back under the table, placing it on Abby's thigh.

Instantly she pushed his hand away in disgust. "If I leave with you voluntarily, you'll give me your word of honor, to leave Cedar Creek. You will not harm Rebecca, Max or Josh ever?"

She scooted as close to the wall as she could get, away from him. Wesley's word of honor was almost worthless, but she didn't see any other options at this point. Somehow, he had done it again, trapped her, dragging her back into the pit of despair.

"That's the deal, you in exchange for the three of them. I have other things also to discuss with you, my dear. I needed to come up with a way to get you out of town. A way in which that pesky sheriff and nosy reverend would leave us alone."

Abby was barely listening to him. Tears threatened to flood her face. She was defeated. How had this happened? She was so happy only yesterday. Today she was headed to purgatory. Putting her hands up to cover her face, she began to sob.

Almost not able to speak, her words were barely audible, "I will go freely, why would they need to follow?" Old familiar feelings overtook her. Despair and sorrow fought for control of her soul. All of her peace was stripped away. Her hopes, dreams, and happiness were crushed under Wesley's feet.

"I almost forgot to mention one more thing. The most important detail of all. You're invited to a wedding tomorrow, at the jailhouse. Sheriff Cole is going to perform the ceremony. It will be a good opportunity to tell your lawman goodbye. You can explain to him that you are leaving him for a much richer and better-looking man. Me, of course!"

"I don't want to go to a wedding, or see Josh." She couldn't face him. Shame and heartbreak overwhelmed her. It was her life in exchange for three innocent ones. It was because of her they were all in danger in the first place. She wished she had never set foot in Cedar Creek.

"Let me go back to my room and collect a few items." Tears still streamed down her face. She didn't know which hurt worse, being forced to be a girl of the night or leaving Josh forever.

"Stop crying like a baby, you're creating a scene." He pulled a white handkerchief from his shirt pocket, shoving it into her hand.

"Wipe your face, it's very unbecoming to see you act so childish. I will accompany you back to your room. Collect your belongings, and don't dally. You will be staying in my room tonight, where you can't run away. We will leave Cedar Creek right after the ceremony."

"I said I would leave without a fight. I don't want to see Josh. You win." More tears streamed down her face. Her nose was red, her eyes grew puffy, and she felt ill. Why must he insist on her going to the jail. It was like pouring salt on a wound. She knew Wesley took pleasure in her heartache.

"I spoke to the deputy earlier, before that terrible fire broke out, it's all arranged. The handsome new groom and his bride will ride out of town, as the lawmen wave their goodbyes."

"Who cares if anyone waves to a newlywed couple?" Abby knew Wesley wanted to let Josh know she was leaving with him, rub it in his face.

Wesley received great enjoyment from others misery and misfortune. Abby wondered if a more wicked man existed than Wesley Roberts?

"I'm not going, I refuse. Do what you will with me, but I won't face Josh." Please God, she begged silently. Don't let him parade me around town to hurt Josh.

With the most self-satisfied look, Wesley declared, "You have to attend the wedding my dear, you're the bride."

Chapter 10

Black ashes and mud sloshed under Josh's feet as he walked amid the rubble and debris of what had been the Stables of Cedar Creek. Only a few smoldering coals remained. The worn-out lawman brushed sweat from his brow, smearing more black soot across his dirty face.

He was covered from head to toe with ash. Looking around, Josh saw that everyone else had gone home except Randy, who had stayed to make sure the fire was completely out and all danger had passed.

The last several hours had been physically and mentally hard on Josh. All he wanted to do was take a bath and go to bed. He couldn't remember feeling this wiped out in his life.

With a yawn, he pulled out his pocket watch, checking the time, nearly three p.m. Most of the day was gone, making it much too late for a trip to the jeweler. It was just as well, he was exhausted, another yawn escaped his lips.

Randy walked up beside him, surveying the damages. "The stables are gone, burned to the ground, a complete loss, but thank the Lord that all the animals were saved. It was touch and go for a while. That chestnut mare about done me in, with all her bucking and kicking, but I got her out safe."

"With all of the commotion did anyone say if they knew how the fire got started?" Randy stared at the mess.

"Not that I heard. We may never know. It's a real shame too, in the blink of eye, everything's gone. I'll do an investigation in the morning, but we've done all we can do for now. I'm going home to rest. You're in charge. If you need me, you know where to find me." Josh turned to walk away.

"Wait," Randy called out. "You won't be able to do anything until after nine in the morning. With all the excitement, I almost forgot, you will be officiating your first wedding ceremony.

A gentleman came in early this morning, right before the fire broke out. He made all the arrangements for an eight o'clock ceremony, paid the fee and hastily left. Come to think of it, he's the same man who was sitting beside Miss Gibbs. I wonder who he's marrying?"

Josh cringed inside, thinking of officiating his first wedding. The entire idea made him anxious. He was secretly glad that it was strangers who were getting married. If he messed up in some way, at least he wouldn't have to see the happy couple ever again.

He knew this day would come, but he didn't realize how soon or scared he would be. A grown man, scared to say a few words little words, and to sign a piece of paper. How hard could it be? Fifteen minutes and it would all be over, he could do this!

"Hey, I just thought of something. Why isn't R.J. doing the ceremony?" Maybe there was a way out after all. Maybe the stranger didn't know there was a reverend in Cedar Creek?

"I asked the guy that same question. He said that he didn't believe in God and didn't see eye to eye with Reverend Johnson. He didn't seem to be the kind of chap that wanted to talk or answer any questions."

Randy bent down, picking up a horse shoe off the soggy ground. "Look, this is good luck, I'm going to hang it over my door post." He smiled, as if he had found a treasure or a piece of gold.

"Don't worry Sheriff Cole, Deputy Anderson has everything under control. Go get you some sleep." With a smile, Randy left with his treasure in hand, leaving Josh alone with his thoughts.

It had been a tiring day, Josh would worry about the wedding, the stranger, and Abby tomorrow. A bath and his bed took control of his mind. Within an hour, loud snores could be heard in the back room of the jailhouse, Josh was sound asleep.

***

Her mouth fell open, Abby couldn't believe what she'd just heard. "Bride, your bride? You want to marry me?" The thought of Wesley being her husband was repulsive. Her heart belonged to Josh only, and always would.

"Don't be absurd, I have no desire to marry you, or any woman. I'm only doing this so I can legally take you out of this miserable town, without that sheriff following me for the rest of my life."

"Marriage means nothing to me and neither do you! When I look at you, I merely see two things. A way to earn money in my brothel and a personal maid. By law you will belong to me. You will be bound to obey, serve, and satisfy my needs." He laughed. "I will own you."

Furrowing her brow, Abby crossed her arms in front of her chest. Speaking defiantly, "I won't do it, I will not marry you? There isn't anything you can say or do that will cause me to change my mind. I have agreed to leave with you, to save my friends lives, but marrying you is out of the question." Sounding very sure of herself, she readied herself for a battle of wills.

Without warning Wesley grabbed her arm, pulling her from the table, twisting her arm behind her back until she winched. Placing his other hand over her mouth, he escorted her out the door and down the sidewalk.

Momma Anderson and the waitress were standing in front of the Café, their full attention was on the smoke as they talked about the fire. They didn't notice Wesley pull Abby down the walkway and around the corner.

They quickly arrived at Wesley's room. Opening the door, he threw Abby inside with force. She stumbled forward, falling to the wooden plank floor. Swiftly closing the door, Wesley sprang toward Abby, grabbing a hand full of her hair, pulling her head back with force. Using his free hand, he firmly clutched her around the waist, pulling her up, pressing her against his body.

"I'm going to crush your sheriff's heart and yours all in one act. Then I will enjoy a long, satisfying honeymoon. And you, my pet, will do everything I say. If you don't, I will kill the sheriff and his dog right in front of you." Laughing he continued, "I might, just for fun, gut shoot that mangy mutt. The rotten animal probably deserves it." Bending down, he kissed Abby hard on the lips.

Squirming under his grip, Wesley's lips upon hers, turned her stomach. Pulling his head back with a half-smile, he shoved her away from him, causing her to fall backward onto the floor, landing hard on her bottom.

Stepping forward, putting the heel of his boot on the top of her hand, he pressed down hard. He began to twist the heel of his boot back and forth. Abby could feel the skin rip as tears began to trickle down her face. Not able to hold back, she cried out.

"It hurts, stop, please stop." Abby hated showing signs of weakness or pain. Wesley fed off of them, craved them. She scolded herself for being soft. She'd had five years of freedom and wasn't used to forcing her feelings down. Choking the urge to cry out in agony, she remained quiet.

"You're mine from this moment forward. If you are a good girl, and I mean very good, in every way," he implied what Abby feared most. "I might not have to use the whip as often. But cross me once and I'll peel your hide clean off. Do you understand me?" His icy glare told her that he was absolutely serious. Stepping away, he freed Abby's hand.

"I understand you, Sir." She knew how she was expected to answer and act, submissive and obedient. Rubbing the skin on the back of her hand she noticed that it was bleeding. At that moment in her heart, she knew without a doubt that she would never survive in California.

Bolting the door, Wesley turned to face his prey. Abby's eyes darted around the room. She was trapped, with nowhere to run and nowhere to hide. Her heart began to beat wildly. She knew the look in his eyes, she'd seen it many times as a girl. She felt twelve years old all over again. Fear and panic flooded her, the same way it did all those years ago.

"I'm your master now!" Seizing the frightened girl by the waist, he easily threw her onto the bed. Snatching up the whip that was lying nearby on the floor, he moved close to his target. With wide eyes, Abby bounced off the bed and dashed for the door. The whip cracked against her back as she frantically tried to move the bolt.

A second hit from the leather tip found her flesh, winding around her neck, then across her cheek. Pain instantly surged through her. Laughter sounded from behind her as a big hand took hold of her arm, spinning her around to face the evil that stood glaring at her.

Mocking her, he chanted, "There is no escape, no escape, no escape ever." His bare hands closed in around her neck and began to squeeze. The breath was being choked out of her. She clawed and pulled to free herself, as she gasped for air.

Like a rag doll, the big man flung Abby over his shoulder. Walking toward the bed, he carelessly dropped her on it. A moment later he was on top her, pressing the air out of her lungs with the weight of his body.

Abby tried to scream, but his large hand quickly covered her mouth and nose. She felt faint, everything grew dark as the room began to spin. The world went black, all sounds went silent.

Suddenly there was a knocking sound at the door. "Mr. Roberts, are you in there? It's me, Mrs. Anderson. I heard a terrible commotion coming from inside your room. Is everything ok in there? I've sent for the deputy, he will be here any minute." Mrs. Anderson pressed her ear against the door, listening for a response.

Jumping to his feet Wesley frantically looked toward the door. Soft moans could be heard from Abby as she began to regain consciousness. Partially disoriented she looked around the room and spotted Wesley. Abby heard Mrs. Anderson knocking and calling out for Mr. Roberts.

"Hello, I know someone is in there. The law will be here any minute. If you're a criminal you might as well give yourself up right now." Mrs. Anderson still pressed against the door, listening for the smallest of sounds.

Placing a finger upon his lips, he signaled to Abby to be quiet. Pulling the knife out of his boot, where he always kept it, he waved it around in the air. Silently he moved close to the frightened girl laying on the bed.

In a whisper he spoke sternly. "If you make a sound or call out for help, I will use my knife to carve my name in your hide. Then I will slice your pretty face up so bad that your sheriff won't recognize you. Do I make myself clear?" Abby nodded her head.

Wesley opened the door opened slightly, peeking out. His clothes and hair were disheveled. "Mrs. Anderson, I do apologize. I was practicing my fencing moves. I get so caught up in the sport and can be loud and bump into things. I will try to be quieter." He flashed her one of his most charming smiles at the older lady.

Trying to peek past Wesley and look into the room, Mrs. Anderson replied. "Oh, dear me. With all that commotion, I thought you were being robbed." Randy walked up as his mother was talking about being robbed.

"Does someone need help, Momma? Was there a robbery?" Randy looked at his mother, then to the stranger.

"I apologize, Deputy Anderson. I seem to have gotten your mother a bit worried, but I've explained everything to her. She is a grand lady for worrying about her tenant's welfare." Taking her hand, he placed a kiss on it, he caused the older woman to blush.

"It is, after all, better to be safe than to be sorry these days. There are a lot of unscrupulous people in the world. You can never be too careful. I will be as quiet as a mouse for the rest of the evening. I have a big day tomorrow, as you well know Deputy Anderson. I bid you both a goodnight." With a polite nod, he shut the door, bolting it.

He looked out of the window, making sure both mother and son had left before he spoke. "This town is full of nosy people. I can't wait to leave this miserable place." Approaching Abby, he grabbed her again, pulling her close.

"It looks like I must be quiet or risk that old woman calling the law again. You get in that corner over there" He pointed to the one beside his bed and furthest from the door, "and don't move."

"I'm going to lay down and rest awhile. Remember, don't move or else my knife will spill your blood." Sitting down on the bed, he took off his boots, then laid down. In a very short time he was clearly asleep, as his loud snores filled the room.

Abby placed her hand on her cheek, touching the spot where the whip had made its mark. She wondered if it would leave a scar and how much more damage a knife would do to her face? After a few moments she realized her only option was to flee.

She would die inside if she had to marry Wesley, he would destroy her spirit and soul. That is if he didn't break every bone in her body or rip her to shreds with his knife first.

Abby knew it would be better to live on the run, in fear, than to survive without her soul. It was now or never. Standing, taking a deep breath, she tiptoed toward the door. Her heart beat rapidly while adrenalin surged in her veins. Placing her hand on the bolt, she carefully turned it, releasing the door to open easily. Without a look back, she slipped out the door and crept away in silence.

Chapter 11

The sun slowly slipped lower and lower behind the horizon. Darkness began to blanket the earth rapidly, casting shadows of ominous shapes, as if to warn of an impending doom. Abby hurried toward the church, time was not on her side.

She knew Wesley was a sound sleeper, nevertheless she had no time to waste. She needed to disappear, using the cover of night, hiding all traces of her existence from Cedar Creek and Wesley Roberts forever. This was a double-edged sword that cut at Abby's heart. She would also be leaving Josh, creating a wound in her heart that would never heal.

As she grew closer to her destination, she realized this would be the last time she would set foot in the church. She would never again watch her curtains swaying in the cool evening breeze, see the sun rise from her doorstep or hear another one of R.J.'s sermons. The saddest part about leaving was that she wouldn't see Rebecca, R.J., Max, or Josh again.

Sheriff Cole appeared in her mind. She pictured his bearded face, rugged jaw line, and his dark brown eyes. She could hear his voice, envision the way he walked, and feel the love that he had for Max. Everything about this man melted her inside.

Tears pooled in her eyes. How would she live the rest of her life without the only man she would ever love? Every instinct in her wanted to run to Josh and explain her circumstances. He was a lawman, he would be able to help her. Shame forced those urges away, replacing them with the fear of rejection.

She would rather leave forever than have him know the truth about her past. Abby had told herself, on numerous occasions, that Josh would understand. He wouldn't love her any less, despite her tainted past.

Running away now was proof that she didn't really believe that deep down inside. By sheer will power she forced herself to not dwell on what she knew she couldn't change.

Arriving at the church, she entered her room without delay. Abby had hidden a small amount of money under her dresser in a stocking. If she was to have any hope of successfully escaping the wickedness that undoubtably awaited her in California, her survival depended on that money.

It had become completely dark outside, making it hard to see inside. Abby swiftly lit the oil lamp, which cast a soft glow throughout the room. Sitting down at her simple wooden desk, she pulled out a piece of writing paper from a neat pile, placing it in front of herself, she picked up a pen and began to write.

Reverend Johnson,
It is with great sadness and emotional distress that I write you this letter. So much has happened since we last spoke. I find myself in the most urgent of circumstances, and have concluded that I must leave Cedar Creek at once. I know this is forcing you to find a new teacher on short notice. I would not leave unless it was urgent. I assure you that it is a matter of life or death, my death in fact. Please accept my sincerest apology.
I feel terrible about asking this, but I am in desperate need of two favors, that I am in no way capable of repaying. I am asking, if possible, would

you return the trunk that is in my room to my mother Grace Gibbs. It is a precious heirloom, a family treasure. I'm sure my father will reimburse any cost you might incur.

The other thing I ask is for Josh to never know of this letter or about my past with Wesley. I want to believe that he would understand and forgive me, but I can't bear the thought if he didn't. I know that I was only a child and it was in no way my fault. Even so, I feel ashamed. Josh deserves a better woman than myself.

Tomorrow Wesley plans to marry me. Not because of any love, but to punish me. It's his way to leave town legally, with me at his side. If I refuse, he has threatened to trick Rebecca in going to California with him. Once there he will force her to work in his brothel. He's also going to kill Max and Josh. It's a threat that he will follow through on, and enjoy doing it. The extent of Wesley wicked soul, only God knows.

Innocent lives are in extreme danger because of me. I love each one of them dearly. I would give my life to protect them. I know Josh will not understand what I've done, at first.

His heart will be crushed when I marry another man and equally as hurt if I disappear from Cedar Creek. It pains me beyond words to leave him. Josh will see what I've done as abandonment or betrayal. In reality, I'm dying inside so he can live.

I hope now you will understand why I must leave tonight. It is my last hope of saving those dearest to me. I want to thank you for making me feel welcome, showing the love of God, and for standing up against Wesley for me. I will miss you terribly.

Your friend always,
Miss Abby Gibbs

Neatly folding the letter in half, she rose from her desk. Taking a couple of steps to the dresser, she bent down to retrieve the hidden stocking from beneath it. As she knelt on the floor, the torn scarf pieces caught her attention.

Pausing, she carefully picked up each piece. Pulling them against her chest, she closed her eyes briefly. She wondered if her life was worth living. She was losing everything and everyone dear to her.

Taking a deep breath, Abby knew now wasn't the time to feel sorry for herself. She shoved the torn pieces of material into her dress pocket, then leaned forward and collected the hidden stocking. She placed them in the opposite pocket as her Bible. She stood to her feet; it was time to go. Picking up the oil lamp, she headed into the sanctuary toward R.J.'s desk.

Seeing the lamp on the corner of his desk, she easily spotted the worn leather Bible that the Reverend kept at the church to study with. Abby had asked him once why he didn't take it home to read and study?

R.J. simply explained that he kept a Bible at home and one at church. He wanted to have God's word near him at all times. His church Bible, as he called it, contained hundreds of hand-written notes on the pages along with paper notes shoved in every nook and cranny. Abby understood and admired his dedication.

Carefully she opened the old tattered Bible. The pages were thin and worn. She placed her note inside, then closed the book. She was sure to leave about an inch of her letter sticking out of the top, well past any of R.J.'s notes.

He would easily see it first thing in the morning. Reaching back into her pocket, she pulled out a piece of her scarf. She placed it on the top of the Bible with a smile. R.J. knew the sentimental value it held and would cherish it as a memento of their friendship.

Time was running out. Figuring about thirty minutes had passed since she left Wesley's room, she didn't have a second to waste. With a quick breath, she blew out the lamp, it was time to go.

She turned to give the room one last look. The moon was shining directly down through the window, landing on the pew where she and Josh sat on Sunday mornings. A smile parted her lips, followed by a twinge of heartache. She wouldn't sit in that spot, or beside him again.

She was wasting precious time. She needed to leave and stop thinking about Josh. Moving to the front door, she opened it just enough to peek outside. Abby surveyed the area, making sure Wesley wasn't outside or coming up the path looking for her. Seeing nothing or no one, she stepped outside.

Night sounds echoed in the distance, making the dark frightening to Abby. The full moon helped calm her somewhat, at least she could see her surroundings. She wasn't fond of walking around in the dark, in the woods, but her other choices were worse. For a brief moment she stood on the step, not knowing which direction to go.

"Lord, help me. I'm scared and don't know where to turn or what to do. I need direction, courage and strength. I don't know why this is happening to me. Lord lead each step I take and keep me safe. Amen." Abby finished her prayer, but didn't hold still long enough for God to answer.

Suddenly she had an idea, a plan in fact. She would head to the Baker farm, which was about a mile straight north of the church. Josh had taken her there once to see a new colt that he was thinking about buying. Abby fell in love with the feisty little animal instantly. It had a white patch of hair on its forehead shaped like a star. The only white on its otherwise all brown body.

She remembered Josh pointing out a deserted road, half a mile past the Bakers farm. It was over grown with tall grass and saplings, barely recognizable as a road at all. He said it used to be the main road to Forsyth, but no one used it anymore because of a land dispute.

A wealthy rancher had bought all of the surrounding land and refused to let anyone cross his property. Josh said it was a legal mess. Eventually a new road was made and ended up being a smoother, easier path to travel.

Abby thought this would be the perfect way out of town without fear of being caught. No one else used the deserted road and if she stayed on the path, she wouldn't have to fear getting lost. With a course settled in her mind, she jumped from the step, hitting the ground in a run. Her heart beat a little faster from the fear of the unknown, but she was free.

Rounding the back of the building, heading north, her body collided with something big. She bounced off, falling backward, landing hard on the ground. The moonlight shown down on her face. As she looked up a dark shape moved between her and the light, creating a black silhouette of a man.

Abby's stomach twisted into knots, her worst nightmare was coming true. She knew all too well what was about to happen. Before she had time to imagine what her consequences may be for running away, a strong hand grabbed her arm, yanking her to her feet. Another hand slapped her hard across the face, forcing her head to turn sideways.

"I told you to stay put." Wesley's angry voice growled. He forcefully clutched her chin in his hand, pulling her face toward him. It felt as if he might break her jaw. Abby struggled to breathe, her head reeling from the slap. Reaching up she grabbed Wesley's hand, trying to free herself from his grip. He squeezed harder, not letting her get away. Fear shot through her, he was going to kill her then and there.

Frightened for her life, she fought with everything in her. With as much strength as she had, she kicked and clawed at his flesh. She felt the warmth of his blood under her fingernails as she scratched his forearm.

His hand shot off of her chin as he yelped out in pain. "You little witch. You're going to pay for that. How dare you make a mark on me."

His voice more volatile than she had ever heard it before. Instantly realizing that she was no longer under his hold, she bolted away. She was much smaller than Wesley, but she was quick. If she could make it to the timberline, she had a chance of losing him in the woods.

The cracking sound of his whip caught her ear. Not pausing to look back, she pushed her legs to move faster. The timberline was nearing rapidly. Adrenaline surged through her, only a few more feet to go, she was going to make it.

Stinging pain hit her back as the whip made contact. Abby screamed, not from the pain but from the surprise that Wesley was close enough to hit her with the whip. Deep inside, her hopes of freedom were diminishing.

A second hit was felt on the back of her leg. Thankfully her dress shielded her from most of the blow. Reaching the edge of the woods, she darted in, hiding in the dense shrubbery. Maybe he wouldn't see where she went.

Crouching down she crawled behind a thick pile of briers and brush. She held her breath and listened, not a sound was heard. Not any of the tree frogs that normally sung at night, not the usual sounds of crickets chirping, even the wind was dead calm. It was as if all the forest was waiting to see the outcome of her fate.

Abby didn't move a muscle. She strained to hear even the smallest of sounds. If Wesley was out there, and he was, she should be able to hear his footsteps. Hear a stick break, leaves shuffle, something she thought. Maybe he had gone in the other direction. Was it possible that she may get away? A tiny spark of hope resurfaced.

Wesley was a smart man, she didn't underestimate him for a minute. If he knew where she was hiding, he would have grabbed her already. But he wouldn't give up, he'd stay in the woods all night if he had too and Abby knew it.

Five minutes passed, then ten, and soon thirty. Her chances for freedom were increasing. Wesley must not know where she was hiding. Deciding not to move, this would be her bed for the night. The hard ground and a few leaves never felt so good.

Her senses were heightened, being alert was important. As the night hours crept by, she grew sleepy. This was not a time to let her guard down. She must stay awake! Another hour passed. Not a questionable sound was heard. Nothing other than normal night sounds.

An owl hooted in a neighboring tree, a coyote howled in the distance, and the trickle of the nearby stream was soothing to Abby. She thought those types of sounds would frighten her, but they did the opposite. They gave her comfort, made her feel not so alone.

As the night hours grew later and later, her eyelids became heavy. As she slowly closed them, she told herself that it would only be for a few minutes. What would five minutes hurt?

Quietly, she curled up in a fetal position. In no time, Abby was completely relaxed, as the soothing sounds lulled her into a deep sleep. She didn't hear the rustling of leaves or the shuffling of footsteps that drew closer and closer.

Chapter 12

    Flipping his silver pocket watch open, Josh checked the time, eleven p.m. Lying on his cot in the back room of the jail, he was wide awake and somewhat restless. Mindlessly, he watched the shadows being cast on the wall from the oil lamp as they flickered throughout the room.

    It had been a long day, so why wasn't he asleep, he wondered? Josh couldn't seem to quiet his mind, as endless thoughts about the day's events paraded one after the other in his mind. Nothing had gone as planned, disappointment filled his heart.

    He should have a wedding ring in his possession and be planning his marriage proposal to Abby. How could he ask her to marry him now, without a ring? This was a setback he wasn't prepared for. He'd have to wait, who knows how long, before he could get to the jeweler. More worry bombarded him, maybe it was sign that he shouldn't get married?

What did he have to offer her? He wasn't a rich man, far from it, having only a meager savings. She might laugh if she knew the amount. Abby was accustomed to expensive things and lived in a fine house on the Gibbs ranch, while Josh called the back room of a jail his home. What woman would want to live in a jail?

He imagined Abby at the Gibbs ranch, seated at a long dining table adorned with fine china and a white linen table cloth. Various meats, sour dough rolls, green beans, mashed potatoes and gravy filled the table. After the family had finished the main course, he imagined that dessert and coffee were brought to them by their maid. Josh knew he would not be able to afford any of those things.

Dwelling on Abby's childhood riches wasn't doing him any good. What he needed to do was concentrate on what he could provide for her. At first, his mind was blank. Suddenly it dawned on him of how much he actually did have to offer.

First and most importantly, he loved her deeply. He knew he would do everything in his power to protect her, that he was an honest God-fearing man, and already had a family pet. Abby had a soft spot for animals and she loved Max, this was a plus in Josh's book.

"Yes, a good catch, if I do say so myself." Josh smiled. He may not have wealth, but he had things to give her after all, things money couldn't buy. His mind was made up, he was going to marry Miss Abby Gibbs. But what about the ring?

When would he get a chance to take a trip to the jeweler? It might be days or weeks. It was harvest season, acres and acres of corn needed to brought into the barns. Many farmers didn't have enough help to get in their harvests.

Josh volunteered every year to help gather in the crops. He worked from sun up to sun down. It was hot, back breaking work. Some days he would go home, straight to bed, too exhausted to eat supper.

It was a busy time of year. Josh hardly had time to sleep or eat, let alone leave town for an entire day. The more he considered how long it would be before he could ask Abby to be his wife, the more he knew that he didn't want to wait another second.

He knew that no one is promised tomorrow and life is too short to waste time. His heart quickened and pulse raced. Why should he wait for some day in the future to propose, or for a ring? He'd ask her tonight, right now.

He loved her and he would tell her so. Now was the time. He slipped into his boots, put on his hat, and gun belt. Josh headed for the door. Max jumped up, ready to go, right on his owner's heels. Looking down at his faithful companion, Josh spoke to his dog.

"It's okay boy, you stay here. Hold down the fort." Max turned his head sideways, wagged his tail, and stared at his master.

"Lay down boy, it's ok, you stay here." Josh rubbed his dogs furry head. Max wagged his tail again and sat down. As if understanding Josh's command, Max slowly laid down with a small whimper, then looked up at his owner.

"I know boy, you want to come too, but somebody needs to guard the jail. It's an important job. If someone comes in with an emergency you come fetch me. You're the deputy on duty, I need you to stay."

He rubbed the dog's head lovingly. Thuds from Max's tail beat against the floor. Josh laughed, causing his dog to wag his tail faster sending thumping sounds echoing throughout the room. Max lowered his head to rest it on his front paws.

Seemingly satisfied to stay like Josh asked, he closed his eyes, as if very sleepy.

Josh laughed again, "Well, I didn't have to twist your arm to stay in bed." With a chuckle, he went to door, looking back once more to check on his dog, who still lay resting with his eyes closed. Josh pulled the door closed. Taking a few steps to the edge of the boardwalk, he paused to look up the hill toward the church. He considered what he was going to do if she wasn't awake? If he tapped too lightly, she might not hear him. If he beat on her door, it could frighten her, definitely not a good way to start off a marriage proposal.

The more the thought about it, the more he began to get cold feet. Perhaps going up there in the middle of the night wasn't such a good idea.

Before he knew it, he was half way up the path headed to the church. As he approached something caught his eye. The door to Abby's room was open. The room was completely dark, deserted looking.

Josh felt in his gut something was wrong. Ignoring his feelings, he tried to be logical, perhaps she needed to go to the bushes for a few minutes. Or possibly, like him, she couldn't sleep and went for a walk.

Hoping she would appear any minute, he waited, scanning the area for her, but seeing no one. Thankfully the moon was fairly bright, making it easy for him to spot any movement. After nearly ten minutes, real concern began to set in.

As he looked around, something inside him felt uneasy, as if evil lurked in the shadows, watching him. He was a grown man and not scared of the dark, was he?

The lawman inside him took over as he hurried to the open door. Stopping before entering, he cautiously, slowly peeked into her room, finding it was empty. Next Josh headed to the sanctuary, no one was there either. Stepping back outside Josh listened, for what he wasn't sure. An eerie quietness hovered in the air.

Was his mind playing tricks on him or was there something wicked nearby? Did it have Abby? Was she hurt? Could she be lying in the woods injured? Danger, danger screamed in his ear.

He had to find her. The lawman in Josh took over. He instinctively headed for the thick woodland that crowded the hillside behind the church. Soon he stood facing the edge of the darkened forest. Before he moved any closer, a noise caught his attention.

Leaves rustled, a twig snapped, more leaves being shuffled. Josh didn't need to guess what was making the sound. Someone or something was walking in those woods and whatever it was, it was almost close enough to breathe on him. Taking a step backward, drawing his gun he pointed it straight ahead.

Against all hope he softly called out Abby's name. His instincts told him that whatever was out there wasn't good. What if he was wrong? What if it was Abby, and she needed him? Again, he called out for her. Suddenly the noises stopped, no more than a few feet away.

It was not what Josh wanted to hear, the steps began again, drawing closer and closer, stopping directly in front of him at the edge of the timberline. Josh held his gun steady with a cocked trigger. Whether wild animal or human, he was ready. Taking another step backward, he called out.

"Who's there? Come out with your hands up." Silence hung thick in the air. Josh didn't move, his eyes trained straight ahead.

"Sheriff Cole, I presume." A male's deep voice spoke from the shadows.

Josh held his ground, this person set sent cold chills down his spine.

"Whoever you are, step into the light where I can see you, with your hands up." Josh held his revolver straight ahead. A dark form emerged from the shadows. As the man came forward, he soon stepped into the moonlight.

Josh recognized him instantly. It was the same man who was sitting beside Abby at the café earlier. Josh didn't like how things were playing out one bit. Abby was missing and the last person seen with her was now stalking around in the dark outside her home.

"What are you doing out here and where is Abby?" Josh's voice sounded part concerned and part matter of fact. He didn't like playing games or people who broke the law. The lawman in him didn't trust the stranger at all. Josh watched the other mans' body language, especially his hands. If the mystery man went for his weapon, it would be the last time. Josh was fast, the other man didn't have a chance.

"My apologies sheriff, please excuse my poor manners. I know who you are, but I've not introduced myself to you. I'm Wesley Roberts, a business man from California. I'm in town to collect something that belongs to me. I will be leaving in the morning." Wesley spoke calm, clear words, as if he didn't have a care in the world. He extended his hand as Josh reluctantly shook it. Everything about this man set off warning bells in Josh.

"Mr. Roberts, most people don't roam around in the woods at night. What are you doing out here?" It didn't go unnoticed that Wesley didn't mention Abby or show any concern that she was missing.

"You are correct Sheriff, they do not. This is a first for me, let me explain. As I mentioned, I am a businessman from California. A very wealthy one. I have come to your charming town to collect something that belongs to me, then I will be on my way…" Before he could finish his sentence, Josh interrupted him.

"To collect what exactly? And, why are you walking behind the church at night?" Nothing about this situation seemed right. Josh worried about Abby's safety, but the daunting question remained, where was she? Josh saw a flash of anger in Wesley's face. What was this man not telling him?

"You see Sheriff Cole, I'm in Cedar Creek to collect my bride. She is an exceptional woman. We have known each other for many years, since she was a young girl at the age of twelve.

She wasn't much too look at back then, but she sure did grow up with curves in all the right places. She's the type of woman a man would kill for." Wesley paused, feeling the handle of his gun that sat on his hip. Josh's eyes followed his every move.

Ready to shoot if he had to, Josh kept a steady aim on the man. Wesley went on talking about his future bride but with vulgarly. Josh thought it offensive and in bad taste to talk about his bride in such a manner, but it wasn't his place to correct the groom to be.

Wesley went on, 'We are to be married in the morning, by you sheriff, at eight a.m. I arranged it yesterday with your deputy. Everyone knows getting married is a big step in a man's life. I couldn't sleep and felt the need to take a walk to calm my nerves."

"Before I knew it, I found myself behind the church. That's when I heard a noise that caught me off guard, so I jumped into the brush to hide. Then I could see what or who might be sneaking up on me. There are all kinds of crazy people in this world sheriff. I had to be careful."

"A person can never tell what type of criminal or mad man might be roaming around under the cover of darkness. That's when you called out and I knew it was safe to come out."

Josh listened to Wesley ramble on and on with his story. The lawman in him wasn't buying it, but didn't have any proof that the man was lying.

"Pardon me for asking sheriff, did I hear you calling a woman's name? Is everything alright? Is there a woman in danger? It certainly isn't safe for a female to be out alone. A wild beast might get a hold of her. One never knows what could happen." Wesley's face was emotionless, unable for Josh to read.

Against his better judgment Josh asked, once more, if Wesley had seen Miss Gibbs on his walk. Instantly the countenance of the stranger changed, appearing agitated or angered. A few seconds later it was gone and the unreadable face returned. It happened so fast Josh wondered if he had imagined it.

"Did you notice if the side door of the church was open when you walked by earlier? That is the entrance to Miss Gibbs quarters." Josh had to ask, if this man had anything to do with Abby's disappearance he needed to find out.

Putting a finger to his chin in thought. "I believe it was closed. I didn't notice anything amiss sheriff. I can help you look for her, two sets of eyes are better than one." He waited for the lawman's response.

"Miss Gibbs is not in her room or anywhere nearby the best I can tell. I worry that something may have happened to her. You are right, another person searching would be helpful." Josh didn't trust Wesley but could use help in his search.

"I have a dog that I bet can sniff her out. He's got the best nose around and he loves Miss Gibbs. I'm going to run back to the jail and get him. I do have to ask that you accompany me back to town. If there is any foul play involved, I can't have you out here alone, possibly in harm's way."

Josh wasn't worried about his well-being, he only wanted to keep the man in his sight. With his mind on Abby, Josh holstered his gun and turned to head back to the jail, expecting the other man to follow.

Wesley pulled his gun silently from its resting place on his hip. Raising the revolver, he took careful aim, straight at the back of the sheriff.

Chapter 13

Startled and slightly disoriented, Abby woke to the sound of voices. Afraid of being discovered she held as still and silent as possible, listening. It didn't take long to recognize the voices of Josh and Wesley. Being too far away to hear completely what they were saying, she decided to move closer.

Careful not to rustle any leaves or snap any twigs underfoot, she crept gently toward the two men. As she approached the edge of the woods, both men came into view.

Her eyes widened when she heard Wesley speak about his bride, one worth killing for. Josh seemed to be disinterested in Wesley's bride, changing the subject to ask questions about the missing girl. Not surprising to Abby, Wesley lied, with his usual false charm.

It was too risky to continue to hide in the woods, she needed to find a new place to take cover and stay out of Wesley's sight. Peering up at the full moon, she knew that walking to the Baker farm was no longer an option. She could be seen too easily.

Any other time Abby would have been enchanted by the beauty of the world covered with shimmering moonbeams, but not tonight. If she dared to leave the shelter of the timber, Wesley would surely spot her. It was a miracle that he hadn't found her already.

If she ran to Josh for help, Wesley would surely kill them both. Everything inside of her told her to go to him anyway, jump into his arms, the arms of safety. Smiling, she felt a small spark of hope. Wesley's face appeared before her eyes. Fear of him immediately rushed in, taking complete control of her.

She needed to leave Cedar Creek and Joshua Cole forever. As she frantically searched her mind for any idea of what to do next, her eyes landed on the church. Both men knew she wasn't inside. They probably wouldn't look for her again there. She realized this was the answer that she was looking for, but how would she sneak past the men?

Josh's voice caught her attention, saying he was going back to get Max. When he turned to walk away, Abby was horrified to see Wesley draw his gun and point it directly at Josh's back.

Quickly looking around, Abby grabbed a rock about the size of her fist. She hurled it into the woods are far as she could. It landed with a loud crashing thud echoing throughout the still of the night in all directions.

The unexpected noise caused both men to spin around. Josh saw that Wesley had his revolver drawn and pointed toward the timberline. Walking up beside him, Josh drew his gun as well. Both men had their full attention directed away from Abby and in the direction of the crash in the woods to her far left. This was her chance. She darted out from her hiding place and ran for the cover of the side of the church building, out of the men's view.

Breathing heavily, she carefully peeked around corner, praying that she hadn't been seen. Both men were still focused toward the timber. Seizing the opportunity, she hurried back inside the church, to the safety of her room. She closed and bolted the door behind her.

"Do you see anything?" Josh whispered.

"No, the brush is too thick." Taking a step forward Wesley added, "I'll go take a look. You stay here, in case someone tries to run out." Wesley stepped away, slowly moving into the darkness of the brush and thick trees. Josh didn't like being told what to do, he was the sheriff and gave the orders.

Forcing down his pride, he didn't argue. Besides, if it was a bear or mountain lion, Wesley could be their midnight snack instead of him. As he stood, waiting for any movement or sound, he ran the possibilities over in his mind. Was it a wild animal, maybe it was a coon hunter or could it be Abby?

Worry shot up inside of him, like a prairie fire. Where could she be? Was he looking in the wrong places? Question after question flew in and out, only ceasing when he saw Wesley returning. Josh was done wasting time, he was going to fetch Max and get the search started.

Not bothering to whisper Wesley spoke with a gruff voice, "I didn't find anything or anyone. It must have been an animal or maybe a dead tree branch falling."

Josh saw another flash of anger in Wesley's eyes when he spoke, disappearing instantly, just like before. Why did this man set off warning bells in him? Josh's gut told him something was wrong, deadly wrong as an uneasy feeling washed over him. It felt like a looming thunderstorm threatening to destroy everything in its path. Gripping his gun, a bit tighter, Josh addressed Wesley with authority in his voice.

"Let me see you to your room Mr. Roberts. It's my duty to keep the town's people safe. You shouldn't be out here in the middle of night alone." Josh decided that Wesley's help was no longer needed. He could cover more ground, faster, if his full attention was on searching. Keeping an eye on Wesley would slow him down, not to mention his gut said Wesley was trouble.

To Josh's amazement, Wesley holstered his gun and walked beside him toward town without a word. As they rounded the side of the church, both men could see the door to Abby's room was now closed.

Relief flooded through Josh. Abby must be safe in her room. He was about to hurry over to knock on her door, but something stopped him dead in his tracks. He saw Wesley's eyes were narrowed, his jaw clenched tight, and both of his hands where clinched into fists. Josh didn't know what was going on, but he wasn't letting this man get anywhere near Abby.

Wesley suddenly spoke, "I do hope you find your teacher, Sheriff. I hate to leave you all alone in your search, but it is very late and I have a big day coming up. I need to get some sleep. I bid you a good night." With a nod he hurried toward the diner.

Josh decided to follow him, staying out of sight. He watched Wesley go into his room behind Anderson's Café and close the door. Josh wanted to hurry back to the church, but a voice inside of him said to stay put. He wasn't sure why he was to stand guard outside Wesley's room.

Abby was back in her room so Josh felt he could relax and focus on why Wesley was sneaking around. The more he tossed the night events around in his head, out of nowhere, Josh heard in his spirit, that man is pure evil.

"Evil?" Josh said out loud, surprised by his own thoughts. "Lord forgive me, I don't know this man and I'm accusing him of being an evil person." He felt a tinge of guilt. Before he could explore his feelings the door to the rented room creaked open, as Wesley stepped out. Josh watched, unseen from the shadows.

Wesley stepped far enough out of his room, onto the boardwalk, where the moon illuminated him. Josh could easily see that he was holding a whip in his hand and looking toward the church. If Josh didn't know it before, he knew it now. Wesley had bad intentions for Abby. His gut was right all along, this man was beyond dangerous.

The crack of the whip, caused Josh to jump. Wesley's eyes shot toward Josh. The sheriff knew he'd been seen. He pulled his gun and stepped out of the shadows to face Wesley. Though several yards apart, both men stood staring at each other, not moving.

Josh saw how fast this man had drawn his gun back at the timberline, but he wasn't backing down. If Wesley wanted to get to Abby, he would have to go through him first. Squaring his shoulders, Josh stood his ground.

Wesley stood, clenching the whip in his hand, glaring at the sheriff. Mumbling under his breath something Josh couldn't hear, he turned and stomped back into his room, slamming the door behind him.

***

"Why? Why? Why?" Abby chanted over and over. "Why did you do such a foolish thing and shut the door? Wesley would never have known I was here if I had only left it open. Abby how stupid you are." She harshly scolded herself repeatedly.

Curled up in the corner of her room with both doors and the window locked, Abby stared off into the darkness of her room. A week ago, she felt secure and happy. But now, a few short days later, she had never felt so trapped and in danger in all her life

Would she be able get out of town alive? Wesley didn't allow anyone that crossed him to live. She was as good as dead and she knew it. What she feared most was that he would kill Josh and Max, and make her watch. She couldn't have their deaths on her conscience.

She loved them both and had no choice but to find a way to save them, even if it meant sacrificing her own life. She could go to Wesley and beg, offering to willingly serve him for life. She'd promise never to run away, or put up a fight, and do anything he asked of her. She knew what that entailed, causing her stomach to twist in knots.

"Why God? Why did you let me come here, fall in love, then let the devil find me?" She began to sob from the depths of her heart. Curling up into a fetal position she cried until the tears would no longer come, until she felt numb. She had to find a way to save Josh and Max without getting herself killed.

She remembered that Wesley often forced her to beg, grovel, and plead when he used the whip or visited her room at night. He fed off of her fear and pain. She needed to convince him that she saw the error of her ways. That she was sorry and wanted to go back to California with him.

It would be a huge risk. He might kill her on sight or beat her to a pulp, but it was her only hope. Her hands trembled, as she pulled the cover from her bed, wrapping it around her. Pulling it over her head, as if to hide, she began to weep softly. It was over, her life was over.

She knew by this time tomorrow Wesley would have her under his control, forever. He would punish her with his whip, his weapon of choice. When he was extremely angry, he would tie a piece of glass on the tip of the leather.

Beyond a shadow of a doubt, Abby knew that he wouldn't be satisfied until her flesh was torn to shreds and her blood ran red.

Chapter 14

Since it wasn't light outside yet, Abby could barely see the latch on the door as she reached for it. Her hand trembled and she quickly pulled it back. Did she dare go through with this? Did she have the strength to follow through on her plan? She had been awake all night, suffering from heartache, feelings of despair, but most of all worry.

Abby paused as she thought of her restless night. She was too frightened to sleep and time seemed to be dragging by. She lay awake, intently listening for the smallest of sounds, wondering if Wesley was prowling outside her door. Would he attack her while she slept? She didn't want to take the risk and close her eyes, or let her guard down.

As the night slowly crept onward, and after much consideration, Abby came to a horrifying conclusion. There was the only one way to save her friends. She must return to Wesley and give herself up. She tried to convince herself to run and never look back, but Josh's face kept popping into her mind. She imagined him witnessing his beloved dog being murdered right before his eyes, and it would be all her fault.

Then she imagined Wesley pointing a gun at Josh's back, or him staring down the barrel of a revolver, or feeling the cold blade of Wesley's knife as it plunged into his heart. Scenario after scenario played out in her mind, none of which ended well for Josh.

All of this left her feeling destined to give herself up. She would throw herself at the wicked man's feet and beg for his mercy, promising to never run from him again. She would vow to be his slave for the rest of her life. It was a risky plan; her life might be snatched away this very day.

Abby knew the wrath of a wild man, having faced it many times as a young girl. She recognized the pleasure he received from inflicting pain on her. She was scared to face him but had to try pleading with him for another chance. If she chose to run now, it would haunt her for eternity. Innocent blood shed would be on her hands.

The sun was trying to peek over the horizon, soon to cascade its warm, golden rays across the land. She wished time would stand still. She wasn't prepared for what this new day may bring.

Abby decided that it would be better to stop stalling, and get it over with, because Josh might come looking for her at first light. She didn't want him in harm's way or trying to stop her. If she was to save him, she needed to do it now.

Wesley usually slept until eight o'clock, only because he had been out late drinking or gambling the evening before. She wanted this morning to be the same. If she woke him from a sound sleep, he might be groggy and disoriented, giving her the slight advantage of surprise. She paused, saying a short prayer for protection and that Wesley would let her live and accept her offer. She worried he might beat her within an inch of her life, or worse. She would soon find out.

Squaring her shoulders, she took a deep breath, as if to summon as much courage as possible. Silently she reached for the latch and slowly began to open the door. Her chest felt tight, her heart was racing, and her knees felt weak. All she wanted to do was turn around and run. "Abort, abort! Abort mission," screamed in her ear. Ignoring her instincts, she continued.

The door of Wesley's room made a slight squeak as it swung all the way open. The early faint light of dawn flooded inside, spreading across the room. She didn't dare step inside the lion's den. She could still run away if things went bad, and they may in a hurry. With one snap of Wesley's whip, he could drop her to her knees, or he could pull out his gun and start shooting.

As her eyes began to adjust to the low light inside the room, she could see a form of a man, Wesley, lying on the bed with his back to her. This was her last chance to change her mind, she could easily meet her maker in the blink of an eye.

A soft prayer escaped her lips, "Lord have mercy on my soul. I don't want to die, but if it's your will, I am ready." Choking back the urge to retreat, she took a slight step inside.

Without warning a deep voice spoke from out of the darkness, shooting a wave of panic into Abby's heart.

"You will never see another dawn and neither will your friends!" As fast as lightning, Wesley sprang to his feet, grabbing Abby by her arms. He pulled her inside. Using his foot, he kicked the door shut, not letting loose of his prize.

Morning light was beginning to saturate the room exposing Wesley's face clearly. His eyes glared at her, and his lips were pressed together as he clenched his teeth. Abby believed if Wesley was a dragon that he would be breathing fire down on her right now, not stopping until nothing was left of her but ashes.

Using the back of one hand, Wesley slapped her across the face, so hard it spun her head sideways. As she righted herself, his fist made contact with her eye, knocking her off of her feet. She lifted her hands to cover the eye and began to cry. If she didn't think fast, she was as good as dead.

"I came back. I'm sorry that I ran away. I was scared. I will go with you freely now. We can leave this minute. Please Wesley, give me another chance. I'll do whatever you want, clean, cook, do anything you want. Please don't hurt me anymore. Please." She fell upon his feet, grasping him around the ankles, clinging on for dear life.

"Please, I will willingly do whatever it takes to save my friends and myself. I'm all yours!" Wesley tried to shake her off of him, but she wouldn't be shaken. Reaching down, he grabbed a handful of her hair, pulling her head back. Abby whimpered with pain but held firmly onto his legs.

"Please, I will do as you want and as you say. I will be your slave. I'm begging you, take me and spare my friends. I will never run away again. I will be loyal to you only, forever, I swear!"

Unexpectedly, Wesley let loose of her hair, his facial features relaxed. "You swear? Doesn't your God forbid you to swear or give an oath?" He seemed amused and curious by Abby's vow.

"Do you swear an oath to your God, that what you have said to me is true, and you will not break it? You will work for me, never try to escape or cause me any trouble? You will gladly clean, cook, and be a girl in my brothel?"

Wesley smiled a devious looking grin as he added, "And welcome me into your room whenever I want? Swear an oath to your God, Abby."

Now what was she going to do? If she made a vow to God, she would be bound by it. If she didn't, Wesley would surely kill Josh, Max and her. God help me, what do I do? She needed God to intervene and there was no time to spare.

Before she could answer or knew what to say, a knock came at the door and a voice called out, "Mr. Roberts? It's me, Deputy Anderson. Momma sent me over with a complimentary wedding breakfast for you. Are your awake yet?" The deputy listened for a reply.

Wesley pointed toward the corner behind the door. Abby knew she was to get in it without delay. Letting loose of his legs, she scurried into it.

Wesley placed a single finger on his lips and glared at her. He whispered, "Be quiet or else."

Then he yelled a reply to the man who was waiting outside his room. "Coming Deputy, give me a moment to dress." In a visible rush, he ran his fingers through his hair to smooth it down, tucked in his shirt, and slipped on his boots. Abby watched him put on a false smile, one that she had seen so many times before.

Wesley opened the door, "Good morning Deputy Anderson." Looking down at the plate of food in the man's hands, "Did you say something about breakfast? It smells delicious and I'm famished."

The lawman handed the groom a food tray which held a plate of scrambled eggs, bacon, biscuits, gravy and a glass of milk. "Yes sir, Momma said I better get this to you while it was still hot."

Looking up at the sky Randy added, "It looks like it's going to be a nice day for a wedding, as long as the rain holds off. There are a few dark clouds scattered around, but the sun is still shining. Yes sir, it's going to be a good day."

Not giving Wesley time to speak Randy continued to talk. "Before I forget, Sheriff Cole asked me to let you know that you need to be at the jail a little before eight, to sign a few papers."

Wesley agreed. "That shouldn't be a problem. Thank you again for breakfast." He turned to go back inside but Randy kept talking.

"She must be a special lady? I can't imagine settling down with just one woman. I like variety in my life. Red heads, blondes, brunettes, straight hair or curly hair. I like thin women or ones with meat on their bones, any shape really, heck, I like them all." Randy chuckled.

Wesley replied smugly, "I have to admit, I'm a man who has had my share of women. But you're right, this charming lady is indeed something special. She has the type of beauty that could drive men wild. They would gladly pay to be near her. She's also a hard worker, a fine cook, and a God-fearing woman. She is undeniably a good catch Deputy Anderson."

"She sounds perfect. I believe if I was to ever find me a girl with all those qualities, I would marry her too. Well, Mr. Roberts, I better let you get to your food. I will see down at the jail in a bit." With a friendly smile Randy turned and headed away.

Shutting the door, Wesley instantly began to devour the tasty food, not offering Abby so much as a crumb. "You know, what I said to the deputy made me think. Men would pay a high price for you. I wouldn't have dreamed all those years ago, when you were young and so plain ugly, that you'd ever have blossomed so nicely." Setting the plate on the bed, he walked over to Abby.

Pulling her to her feet, he then pinned her in the corner using his body. Lowering his head, he kissed her as his hands roamed over her body. Abby squirmed as she fiercely tried to push him away, but she was not strong enough. She tasted the bacon on his lips. It turned her stomach; he disgusted her.

"You do indeed have all the right curves that men would be willing to pay a high price for. I'm thinking a sampling of what I'll be selling is in order." He seized Abby and tossed her onto the bed, sending the plate crashing to the floor.

"Wait, you have to be at the jail soon. Let's wait until the honeymoon. I will make it worth your while, if you wait." She would say almost anything to stop what was about to happen.

Wesley landed on top of her with a heavy thud. He began to kiss her while he tore at her clothing. Abby fought to push him off, but she struggled under his weight. Unable to move, tears began to roll down her cheeks. Wesley was out of control and unstoppable.

Turning her head to the side, away from his face, she started to recite scripture from the Bible out loud. "The Lord is my Shephard; I shall not want. Though I walk through the valley of death, I shall fear no evil…"

"What are you doing. Shut up." Wesley began to grope her again.

"Your rod and your staff comfort me…'

With a loud growl of anger Wesley jumped off of her, and to his feet. "I said shut up. I don't want to hear it." Grabbing his whip, from the top of the bed post, he promptly snapped it into the air.

"Shut your jabbering mouth!" Another crack sounded throughout the room. Abby felt the tip of the leather slash across her lips. It barely made contact, but it was enough to silence her and bring blood. Raising her hand, she gently touched the spot, she could feel it as it bled.

"Let's get one thing straight right now, I will not tolerate your mumbling about God, prayers, or whatever you call them. It's all complete nonsense, there isn't a God! Even if there was, I'm in control here, not him."

As the last word fell from his mouth another knock was heard at the door. Abby could see rage building in Wesley's face. His nostrils flared, his cheeks turned as red as burning embers. His hands closed into fists, he was ready to fight.

"I can't wait to get out of this wretched town. A man can't have a moment's peace. I despise Cedar Creek, and everyone in it!" Another tap at door caused Wesley to close his eyes. He took several deep breaths, in and out, in and out.

Abby watched as Wesley's body relaxed and his features smoothed. Opening his eyes, he pretended to smile as he opened the door to Deputy Anderson holding a plate with two large cinnamon rolls.

"I'm sorry to trouble you again Mr. Roberts. I forgot to bring momma's famous sweet buns earlier. She wouldn't have been very happy with me if I let you miss the best part of your meal." Randy held the plate out for him to take.

Wesley received the plate, holding it up to his nose to inhale the sweet aroma of brown sugar and cinnamon. "They smell delightful, I know I will enjoy them. Please tell your mother thank you for me, in case I don't see her again. It was very kind of her to think of me on this special day. You both have made the start of my morning very memorable, I can assure you." Wesley said a polite goodbye and shut the door.

Cramming his mouth full of sweet bun, it took him only a few minutes to devour the entire thing. He barely took time to chew. "These are the best buns I've ever tasted." Licking the icing off of his fingers he watched the young woman cowering on the bed.

"I can see there will be no way to escape the meddling people around here or take you to California unless we get married." He pointed to the water basin, "Pour some fresh water, then clean yourself up. You look a mess. We can't have you showing up on your wedding day looking like a mangy cat, now can we?" He shoved half of the second roll into his mouth.

"Wedding? We don't need to do that anymore. I will go willingly. We can leave right now if you like." Abby didn't want to leave with him, then or ever. The thought of being married to him, bound for eternity, was a far worse nightmare.

She thought it much like signing her soul over to the devil himself. She wanted to break down and sob but what good would it do? Her crying days were over, it was time to go into survival mode.

She had to retreat into the deepest part of her being. Shut herself off from the rest of the world, shut down her emotions. She wanted to be numb, feel nothing. It was the only way to survive the cruel heartless man that was about to take possession of her.

If Wesley could, he would break her. She vowed inside not to let him. She had survived many years with him once and she could do it again. Her existence would be one of torment and shame, but she wouldn't let him win and steal the only thing she had left, her spirit.

Abby stood, walked to the water basin that was sitting on a small table under the window. Glancing outside she noticed the sky had grown much darker, tree branches were swaying and bending in the wind. Thick black clouds rolled through the sky, a storm was clearly brewing.

Abby thought it fitting, that's how her life was going. Sunny one minute, life couldn't be better. Then without warning, it was dismal and dark, a storm on the horizon.

Without saying a word, she poured a little water into the bowl. A bar of soap had been placed on a hand towel beside the basin. She figured Mrs. Anderson kept items like this in the room for her quests.

Picking it up, the scent of roses filled the air around her, causing her to remember the house on the edge of town with the rose bush planted at the gate. She wished she was there with Josh, instead of trapped alone with Wesley.

Lathering her hands, she began to wash her face. Her eye was tender to the touch, she could feel it was swollen. Being sore, bruised, or hurt would be something she better get used to. This was her life now. No amount of wishing was going to change it. After cleaning her face and hands she pulled the bottom of her dress up to dry her face.

She happened to notice a small mirror hanging on the wall beside the window. She took a step to the side so she could see herself. A purple, puffy eye stared back. It would get worse over the next few days, she had her share of blackened eyes over the years. She told herself to look away, not to dwell on it, they always healed and would look as if nothing had happened in a few weeks. It was her heart that would never be same or heal. Without Josh she would die inside.

Her mind went to God. Why had He let her come to Cedar Creek? Why had He allowed her find true love, only to steal it away so cruelly? Tears threatened, remaining strong she forced them back. As she continued in her thoughts of self-pity and Josh, Wesley busied himself packing his belongings into a saddle bag. As he collected the whip, he looked toward Abby.

"After we are away from Cedar Creek, and Sheriff Cole, you have a long overdue lesson coming to you." Abby watched his temper rise. He pushed past her, grabbing the mirror from the wall. Slamming it into the corner of the table, it shattered it into pieces. Bending down, he picked up a few of the long, narrow, and sharpest pieces.

Looking back to Abby, he spoke in a stern voice, his expression was gravely serious. Holding the pieces of glass up to her face, "You know what I'm going to do with these, don't you girl?"

Her eyes widened, as Abby nodded her head up and down. She knew exactly what he intended to do. Anxiety filled her, what had she done? She had made a lethal mistake, she should never have come back. What was she thinking? God, why did you let me return to him?

Her mind raced, and Wesley knew it, "I see you are remembering all the fun we had the last time I tied glass to the tip of the whip. If you weren't so defiant, you wouldn't need lessons." He laughed, appearing extremely pleased with himself.

"I intend to have my honeymoon and then it's lesson time. I don't know which one I look forward to more." A smile parted his lips. He drew Abby close to him, kissed her, then pushed her away. "Now that you're a woman, you might enjoy my special time."

Abby wanted to grab the soap from the table and wash his taste from her lips. She would rather be ripped to shreds by the whip than let him touch her. She didn't have the nerve to voice her feelings or let him know how he repulsed her. It would only make him angry.

Her only hope was God. Please get me out of this, she prayed silently. I was a fool, I didn't ask you what to do. I thought I could handle it all myself. I realize I was wrong, I can't. Please free me from this man.

Wesley pulled a gold watch from his pocket to check the time. "It's almost eight o'clock. We need to go." Picking up his saddle bag, he shoved the whip and glass into it and tossed it over his shoulder. Taking Abby by the arm, he readied to leave.

"Let's get this sham over with. The quicker we marry, the faster I can leave town." Placing his face directly in front of Abby's, his hot breath hit her face. "You will be my possession forever. No lawman or God can save you." With a self-satisfied look, he pushed her out the door.

High winds crashed into them the moment they set foot outside. Thick, eerie clouds swirled overhead. An occasional streak of lighting flashed through the sky.

"I have to pick my horse up from the boy down the street who has been taking care of him for me." Wesley spoke loudly to be heard over the sound of the wind.

"I'm going to drop you off at the mercantile, to pick up a few things that we will need for the trip back to California. Don't speak to anyone, and if you run, my gun has a bullet with the sheriff's name on it, and his dog's too."

"I won't chase you, I will go straight to the jail and within seconds Cedar Creek won't have a sheriff any longer. I'm sick of you and this town. I hope you've not caused me more trouble than you're worth. You better bring big money girly. You owe me a fortune and I want it all back, with interest."

Abby remained silent for a few moments, then spoke. "I won't try to escape Sir. I will be of great value to you in California, if you give me the chance."

Pausing to gauge Wesley's mood, she added, "What supplies do you want me to get?" Apparently pleased with her response, Wesley gave her a list, along with a few coins to pay for the items.

"Have the clerk put everything in a burlap bag, then tie it shut. Toss it over the back end of my horse, then get yourself inside the jail. Any questions?"

"No sir, I understand." This was how her life was to be. Following orders, obeying to the letter or suffer the consequences. With slumped shoulders, she accompanied him to the mercantile, where Wesley voiced one last warning to her.

"Remember, be a good girl Abby, or…" he pulled his gun from its holster, "Pow, no more sheriff." Acting as if he had shot his revolver, he blew the pretend smoke from the end of the gun barrel.

"And in case you think I've forgotten your little friend, the shop girl, I haven't. One wrong move from you, and she will take your place in California."

Wesley turned and went to collect his horse. Abby, wasting no time, went into the dry goods store. Mr. Anderson welcomed her with a friendly smile and hello. Keeping her head down she avoided as much eye contact as possible. She wondered if Mr. Anderson noticed her eye, but was relieved he didn't comment if he did.

Once her list was complete and sacked up, she paid then swiftly left. She felt rude, but didn't want the shop owner to start asking her questions. Why did she need tobacco, hard tack and why did she have a black eye?

Wesley's horse was already tethered to the railing in front of the jail. Abby took one last look around town. She glanced at the little white cottages, watched people coming and going in their daily routines, she was going to miss this place.

As her eyes roamed around, they landed on the jail. This was the last time she would ever see Cedar Creek, the jail, or Josh. A single tear fell down her cheek. She quickly wiped it away; it was time to get married.

***

Josh looked up to see who was coming into the jail, expecting to see Mr. Roberts and it was. Standing up, Josh held out his hand to shake the grooms. "It's the big day. Congratulations." Josh looked over Wesley's shoulder for the bride but saw none.

"Where's the bride? Did she get cold feet and run away?" Josh laughed. Wesley didn't look amused by his joke. Josh thought he even appeared slightly angered by it.

"I'm only kidding, I'm sure she is a lucky woman to be getting married to a wealthy businessman and live in California." Josh gave Wesley a friendly pat on the shoulder.

"She will be along shortly. She had a few errands to run. You know women, they can't ever be on time. She, no doubt, wants to make a grand entrance." Wesley replied without any emotion. Josh thought he seemed cold, but didn't care, he wasn't marrying the guy.

"It's just as well, I have some papers that need your signature." He motioned Wesley toward his desk. As the groom completed his paperwork the two men made small talk. Randy came into the room just as all the papers were signed. All they needed now was a bride.

Randy said hello to Wesley, then explained that he was to be a witness for the couple. The deputy added his signature beside the grooms on the marriage certificate.

Looking around, he noticed the missing bride. "Where is the future Mrs. Roberts?" Randy asked, still looking around the room as if he missed her somehow.

Just then the door opened and Abby walked inside. She kept her face down and didn't speak. Josh's face lit up instantly as he rushed to her.

"I have been so worried about you. Have you been sick, are you ok?" He wanted badly to throw his arms around her and never let go.

"I'm fine Sheriff." Abby said quietly. Max was asleep in the other room and on hearing her voice came running. His tail was wagging so hard with excitement, it almost knocked her down.

"Ah, Max, I love you too." She happily rubbed the dogs head, bending down to hug him. As if just noticing Wesley, Max moved himself between Wesley and Abby, growling with bared teeth.

"Get that dog away from me Sheriff. I don't want bit." Wesley took a step back.

"Max, come here boy." Josh took hold of his dog's collar and began dragging him toward the back room. The big dog locked his legs, extended his claws and dug into the floor. He didn't want to be moved.

With great effort Josh managed to get him into the back room and shut the door. Max began to bark and howl until Josh yelled at him to be quiet.

"I'm sorry about that. I don't know what got into him. He usually doesn't act like that around people. I think he must have been trying to protect Miss Gibbs, you're a stranger to him. I honestly have never seen him act so vicious before."

Josh's attention returned to Abby. He sensed that something was wrong. She was avoiding eye contact, keeping her face down, and seemed tense. She wasn't wearing her scarf either. He hadn't seen her go anywhere without it.

He needed to find out what was going on but didn't have the time under the circumstances. If Wesley's bride didn't show up in the next few minutes, he would make him reschedule,

He decided after the newly married couple left, he would scoop Abby off of her feet and propose. He wasn't waiting one more day. He wanted to marry the pretty little teacher immediately. He felt so much in love it hurt. He couldn't eat, sleep, or concentrate on anything except her. Ring or no ring, today was the day.

Pushing the thoughts of his own marriage aside, Josh turned his focus on the groom. "Is your bride arriving soon? I have other important matters of business to take care of today. I can't wait much longer. I'm sorry, but if she isn't here in the next five minutes, we will have to make it another day."

Wesley took Abby's hand, pulling her to his side. Lightning streaked across the sky and thunder shook the room, as he replied, "This is my bride."

Chapter 15

A yell escaped Martha's lips as her feet slid out from under her, sending the freshly gathered eggs in her hands sailing through the air and on to the floor, hitting with a splat and cracking open. She landed on top of the sticky mess, leaving her dress soaked with eggs.

Reverend Johnson jumped out of bed, when he heard his wife's scream, and went running into the kitchen to see what had happened. He found his wife sitting in a pile of broken eggs, rubbing her ankle and chanting "Oh dear, Oh dear me."

"What happened? Are you injured?" Rushing to her, he knelt to look for any injuries as he waited for her reply.

"I don't know. One minute I was fixing to make your breakfast and then the next thing I knew I was on the floor. I'm sorry dear, your breakfast is going to be late this morning. Will you please help me up? I may have twisted my ankle." Martha held out her hand for her husband.

Ignoring her hand, R.J. easily scooped the petite woman into his arms. Swiftly, he carried her to the bed, placing her on it. Grabbing the pillow from his side, folding it in half, he elevated her leg.

"Your ankle is beginning to swell, should I fetch a doctor?" Not letting her reply, he added, "And cooking is out of the question. I don't think you need to be on your feet to make breakfast or any meal today. I want you to stay in bed and rest." He carefully turned her foot to the left, then right, then up and down. With each movement he asked if it was painful.

"It hurts a little, but not too bad. I think I'm perfectly capable of fixing a few eggs and a couple of pancakes. Anthony, your being too overprotective, if you ask me." Swinging her legs off of the bed, placing her feet on the floor, she stood. Gasping, as pain shot up her leg, she quickly fell back onto the bed.

With his wife not able to stand, he spoke firmly. "That settles it, you're staying put. I will take care of things around here today." Walking to the water basin, he poured some water into the bowl, picked up the small bar of soap sitting next to it, and carried them to his wife. "You freshen up and I'll bring you something else to wear."

In no time, Martha was in clean clothing and feeling better. R.J. instructed her to take it easy for the remainder of the day. She fussed with him, arguing that she had too much to do. It was laundry day.

All of the dirty linen and clothing were already gathered and sitting beside the wash tub in the kitchen. R.J. confidently assured her not to worry. He could get his own food, do the laundry, and take care of any other chores that needed done.

Martha pleaded her case one last time. She insisted that she could take care of the household tasks herself. "Anthony, there is no need to treat me like I'm helpless. It's just a little sprain." She frowned at her husband.

"There are things that you need to get done. You haven't gone to church to study, or prepared your sermon for tomorrow. It is Sunday you know? The laundry can wait a few days."

"I will have plenty of time to come up with what I'm going to preach on. Maybe I should teach on obeying your husband?" R.J. chuckled as he winked at his wife.

"I don't find the humor in that." Martha crossed her arms and looked away, trying to hide her half-smile. It wasn't long until they were both laughing.

After hours of fetching water, washing, rinsing, and wringing out each item, it was time to hang everything out to dry. Going back inside, he needed to find the clothespins. After a few minutes of looking with no luck, he gave up.

"Who needs clothespins? I'll toss everything over the line and bam, I'm done." Carrying the large basket of bedding over to the clothesline, he didn't give much thought to the dark sky or the wind that was picking up.

Sitting the basket down, he stretched and rubbed his back. "I never knew how heavy wet clothes could be. How on earth does Martha lift this by herself?" He began to toss each item, one at time, across the line. The wind had picked up and was blowing the clothes back and forth.

"At least things should dry fast." Standing back, he looked at the completed job and smiled. "Martha will be proud of me." As the last word fell from his lips, a strong gusty breeze shot through, blowing the majority of the clean laundry onto the ground. Everything, except for one sheet, was covered in dirt, grass, and leaves.

With his shoulders slumped, he let out a sigh, "Well, I can see the use for the clothespins now. Martha doesn't need to know about this Lord, let's keep this between us." Not wasting any time, he began gathering up everything that had fallen to the ground.

"Lord, in case I haven't thanked you lately, I want to now. Thank you for blessing me with such a wonderful wife."

"Are you talking to yourself?" Martha limped outside toward her husband.

"Why are you out of bed?" R.J. hurried to help his wife to the bench in the yard.

Holding her head down, with sadness in her voice, she spoke, "I'm tired of being cooped up. Besides, you do enough around here, without having to do my chores too. I feel terrible about that."

"You know, Martha, I needed to be taught a lesson and the Lord obliged me. After twenty years of marriage, I've not given any thought to how much you do, or how hard you work. I always have clean clothes, food on the table, and a happy home life. I realized today how amazing you are!" He gave his wife a gentle hug.

Martha smiled, "Speaking of work, you need to get a sermon ready. The day is slipping away fast. You haven't had a moment to pray or plan for it. My ankle is feeling better, everything else can wait."

"God's work is more important than anything left undone around here. We have left over roast for supper, so don't worry, now go." She pointed toward the church.

R.J. grinned at his wife, "Yes ma'am!" Kissing her cheek, off he went.

***

Josh looked at Abby, expecting a smile or laughter, this must be a joke. It wasn't the slightest bit funny to him. Abby kept silent with her head down. After several long moments Josh's heart began to sink.

"Your bride? Abby what's going on?" Josh deep down inside was hoping, praying, for her to deny it. She wasn't going to marry another man. Abby remained downcast, as Josh took a step toward her, taking her hand into his. Placing his other hand on her chin, he raised her head to look at him.

A blackened eye stared back. Josh shot any angry glare at Wesley. "What happened to her?" Josh demanded.

His attention returned to Abby, "If this man put a hand on you, I will arrest him… Abby?" Something about Wesley always made Josh feel uneasy. Striking a woman was unacceptable and this made Josh downright angry.

"I didn't lay a hand on her Sheriff Cole, and I take offense to you saying I did. I would never hit a woman, especially the one I'm about marry, my own bride. What kind of man do you think I am?"

Grabbing Abby's arm, Wesley yanked her against him. "I demand we get on with the wedding."

Ignoring Wesley, Josh continued his questioning. "Did he do this to you?" Josh wanted to punch the protesting groom in the eye. He knew that was wrong thinking, but he couldn't control his thoughts, only his actions.

Abby broke her silence, "I was fetching water from outside, tripped, and fell on the bucket. The handle hit me in the eye. I'm ashamed of how awful I look." She pulled her hand out of Wesley's, and took a step away.

Abby met Josh's gaze, "Sheriff Cole, can we please get on with the wedding. It looks like it might storm soon and we need to get going."

"Abby? I'm a lawman, I can protect you. Tell me. I won't let him hurt you?"

In a low tone, Wesley growled, "I told you once Mister, I didn't lay a hand on her. Tell him Abby!"

"Sheriff, I tripped. I am going to wed Mr. Roberts and move to California." She looked directly into Josh's eyes, "Please, let me go."

Josh was taken back, she spoke so coldly, as if she was a stranger. "Abby, don't you know how I feel about you? I'm in love with you. How can you marry another man? Do you love him?" His heart raced, he wanted badly to pull her into his arms or wake up to a bad dream.

Randy stood in the corner of the room, watching, listening, but not saying a word. Josh glanced his way once, sending a silent warning, to stay out of it.

As if uncomfortable, Randy spoke up. "If you folks will excuse me, my father needs me at the store." He left without looking back or another word.

"I'm not fast to anger Sheriff, but my patience is wearing thin. My bride and I insist that you do your lawful duty and marry us immediately, and stop harassing us."

"Abby, do you love this man?" Josh and Wesley both intently waited for her answer.

"Josh... Sheriff Cole, I can honestly promise that I am getting married out of love from the depths of my very soul. There will never be another man that will hold my heart." Not able to hold his gaze, she looked away.

Wesley beamed, "See there, Sheriff, a woman in love, now get on with it."

Josh felt an invisible dagger pierce his heart. How could she be in love with someone else? All he wanted to do was hold her in his arms and pretend none of this was happening. It should be him that kissed her goodnight, him that she woke up beside each morning and him she grew old with.

After a short awkward silence, Josh had no choice but start the wedding. He listened, in agony, as Abby spoke her wedding oath, and couldn't help but notice the groom hurried through his vows, as if they meant nothing. Swallowing hard, Josh almost didn't get the last words to come out of his mouth.

"I now pronounce you husband and wife. You may kiss the bride."

Josh couldn't bear to watch, at the same time couldn't look away. Another man kissing the woman he thought, in his heart, he would spend the rest of his life with. His stomach was in knots, churning, he felt ill.

Wesley put his arms around his new bride, pulling her close to him, as he bent down to kiss her. Abby's body stiffened and she tightened her lips. She didn't act like a woman in love. Anger bit Josh, as he watched Wesley's hand roam over Abby's body. A man shouldn't do that in a public place, and no man should be doing it to Abby. Josh had seen enough.

Turning his back on them, he busied himself with signing the wedding papers. Once done, looking back at them, "Here is your copy of the certificate." He handed it to Wesley. "Congratulations Mr. and Mrs. Roberts." With a forced smile he shook the groom's hand.

"Thank you, Sheriff Cole." Shoving the paper in his jacket pocket he looked at his wife. "Come Abby darling, we had better get moving. We have a lot of ground to cover." Glancing out the window, he frowned. "And by the look of things, a storm is moving in fast."

With lust glistening in his eyes, he scooped Abby up into his arms, "And nothing is going to stop my honeymoon plans!" Wesley hurried out the door with his wife in his arms.

Dark gray clouds were being pushed through the sky by an unnerving, howling wind. It seemed to scream that danger was lurking ahead. Wesley ignored the threatening wind and clouds, as he placed Abby in the saddle and then climbed up behind her. With a snap of the reigns and kick of his spurs, the horse took off in a gallop.

Josh watched as the horse trotted away. Abby left without a goodbye or even a glance back. It was more than Josh could stand. Stepping back inside, he closed the door. Through the small jailhouse window, he watched until the couple were completely out of sight. He felt crushed, witnessing the woman he loved, and wanted to spend his life with, ride away in another man's arms. Covering his face with his hands, falling to his knees, he sobbed.

Chapter 16

Dark clouds hung thick in the air as R.J approached the church. High winds pulled and tugged at his clothing causing him to hold his hat in place. Picking up the pace, he rushed toward the safety of the house of God.

It seemed like the heavens might open up and flood the earth any minute. The second his foot landed on the church step, a single raindrop hit his cheek. Before the latch on the door clicked completely open, rain poured down. Hurrying inside, he went straight to the window and looked outside. It was hard to see anything through the heavy rain, mixed with pea size hail, as it pelted against the glass.

"This looks like a bad storm. I pray Martha is alright at home alone, especially with an injured ankle?" He started pacing around the room walking from one side of the church to the other, then from the front of the room to the back of it. Over and over he paced, praying as he went.

Each time the reverend passed by the window, he took a peek outside. "R.J., get ahold of yourself, it's only a little rain and thunder. It's not the first storm Martha and I have ever been in. Why am I feeling on edge with this one? I've given many sermons on faith. It's time for me to practice what I preach. Lord, help me to trust in you completely!"

Halting in his tracks, R.J. knelt down and continued on with his prayer. "The Lord is my comforter, my strength, my rock, my fortress, of whom shall I fear..."

***

Cedar Creek was an hour behind them when the sky opened up releasing a heavy, drenching rain on the newlywed couple. Abby could feel Wesley's body press against her as he sat behind her on the horse. She wanted to push him away and scream don't touch me.

What was she going to do once she was alone with him? She wished she was dead. Just then a loud clap of thunder caused her to jump. They needed a safe place, out of the storm and fast.

"Wesley, we need to find shelter. It's dangerous to be out in this kind of weather." Abby called out over the roar of the gusting winds.

"What should I do, your majesty, snap my fingers and have a mansion appear?" Wesley shot back angrily. "Stupid girl, of course we need to find someplace dry. Unless you know where that is, keep your mouth shut."

Reaching into one of his saddle bags, Wesley pulled out a full bottle of whiskey. Pulling the cork out with his teeth, he spit it onto the ground. Lifting the bottle to his lips, he drank freely. Small sips at first, but they quickly turned into large gulps. Abby watched as the bottle emptied in his hand as he drank. In a few short minutes it was almost empty.

Neither of them said a word, as they rode onward in misery. Abby couldn't stop the memories of her abusive past, causing her to second guess the choice she'd made. Why had she agreed to marry a man she hated? There must have been a better way?

She should have told Josh everything, he would have protected her. Now she was bound to a heartless, cruel monster for the rest of her life. She tried not think of what he was going to do to her that night. She felt nauseous and her pulse raced as tears streamed down her cheeks, hidden beneath the rain.

God please help me, she prayed, again and again. Maybe God didn't hear her the first fifty times she asked? She knew he did, but fear was taking control of her. Knowing not to let herself go down that path, she tried to turn her attention to the storm.

It was relentless, with no end in sight. The road had turned to thick mud, making travel dangerous. Their horse slipped and stumbled a few times, but always kept his balance. Wesley cursed at the animal, then at Cedar Creek and the rest of the world. He didn't hold his liquor very well, often becoming violent. Abby knew to stay silent, or be punished.

All she could do was continue to pray. Wesley didn't believe in God, but Abby knew better. In the Bible, in God's word, it said that people have not because they ask not. So, she decided to ask for any type of refuge. A tree, cave, old barn, house, anything that could be used for shelter. More importantly, she asked that God rescue her from the man she mistakenly married.

Wesley chugged downed the rest of the whisky. Abby could feel his body tremble against hers, he was shivering. She didn't know how he could be cold, with so much alcohol in his bloodstream. She felt chilled, but nowhere close to the point of shivering.

Wesley was much larger than her, towering over her in the saddle. Most of the pelting hail and rain was hitting his back. He was, unknowingly, a shield for Abby.

Their horse had wondered off of the main road miles and miles back. Wesley was trembling more than before, slouching lower in the saddle, pressing on Abby's shoulders and back to support himself.

She felt Wesley's body begin to sway side to side with the horse's rhythm as it walked. She wished he would lean so far sideways that he would fall off. She would ride on without him, to freedom.

Abby was feeling discouraged, when something caught her eye in the distance. She strained to see through the rain, but it appeared to be a cabin almost hidden in a grove of trees, straight ahead of them.

She yearned for dry clothes and a warm fire. As they moved closer, Abby believed that it was abandoned, with no sign of being lived in. The door hung halfway off one of its hinges, no smoke rose from the chimney, and numerous weeds and brush almost overtook the small oasis.

"Look, a cabin," she pointed straight ahead.

Wesley sat up, dug his spurs into the horse's side, forcing the exhausted animal to move faster. Arriving at the shack, it didn't look very large, possibly a room or two.

There was a covered porch across the front, possibly six feet long. Abby didn't care if the cabin was run down or about the porch, as long as it had a roof and four walls. Wesley jumped out of the saddle, kicking his bride in the back with his boot as he went.

"Stupid girl, get out of my way." He slurred his words, as he stomped past her, gathering the reins of his horse, staggering as he went. He led the worn-out animal under the covering of the porch. Abby knew he didn't care about the animal, just his way back to California.

A flood of thoughts bombarded her. She had mixed feelings about finding this place, she worried that it would come with a high price. She would be alone with a vengeful drunk. A man without a soul. Nightmares, cold sweats, and pain, were her future. Waves of panic soared inside her. She knew this moment would come, but now that it was here, she wasn't ready. She would never be ready.

Without warning, a hand seized her by the arm, yanking her off the horse. "Stop day dreaming, you have work to do." With a shove, he pushed her close to door. "I'm going to take care of my horse."

He started to unbuckle the saddle. His body swayed side to side. Abby thought he might fall over any minute.

"Get inside and build a fire." Reaching inside his saddle bag, he pulled out a few matches, tossing them to her, "Don't waste them, or I'll tan your hide." He glared at her with glossy drunken eyes before he continued tending to his horse.

How would she build a fire with wet matches? To her surprise and relief, when she caught them, they felt dry. Turning she went inside, immediately spotting a fireplace. There was a good size wood pile stacked beside it.

Everything in the room was covered in dust and cobwebs, which meant spiders. Abby loathed spiders. She remembered years ago when Wesley threw a big, black, hairy one in her hair. She had bad dreams about it for months.

The cabin had sparse furnishings, consisting of only one rickety wooden chair, three dirty empty old tomato crates, and the pile of wood. She noticed someone had hung a tattered wool blanket on the wall, covering the window causing the room to be dim.

Walking to the woodpile, she immediately checked for anything scurrying around, happily finding nothing. She collected tiny shreds of kindling, placing them in the fireplace. Next, she added a few small sticks, and lastly the larger pieces.

All the while, she could hear Wesley cursing, slamming things around, and the shuffle of his feet on the floor. She didn't dare look at him. Making eye contact was the last thing she wanted. It was best to keep busy and stay out of his way. She wished she could hide or even run away. She knew that would be foolish, there was nowhere to go.

Retrieving the matches from the chair where she had placed them, her hand trembled as she struck one on the stone and praying it would light. A soft yellow and red flame flickered, sending a tiny ray of light into the room.

Cupping the match with her hand, she carefully laid it on the shreds of wood. Instantly a spark shot up, along with a small amount of smoke. It didn't take long for a few little flames to emerge. Abby gently blew on the fire, until she heard the snap, crackle and popping sounds of the wood.

Wesley carried the horse's saddle in, placing it near the fireplace, then he hung the door back on its hinge. Abby could hear an occasional cough, in between the slurring of his curse words. He was never very handy around the saloon, always hiring someone to do those things, but she was glad he fixed the door.

Risking it, she glanced at him as he was closing the door. His hands were shaking and he looked pale. She couldn't tell if he was sick, drunk, or merely cold.

The fire started to crackle and roar as it burned hotter. The warm, radiant heat was welcomed as she rubbed her hands together near the flames. She stood as close as possible, letting the heat penetrate her wet clothing.

Remembering the Bible in her pocket, she reached inside and pulled it out gently. It was soaked cover to cover. Opening it carefully, she placed it in the chair. She slid the chair closer to fire, but not too close, in case a spark flew out. The warmth and heat would help dry the pages faster.

Unsteady on his feet, Wesley made his way beside her, stopping when he saw the Bible. With a swift backhanded slap, he shoved it off onto the floor.

"Where did that come from? Get it out of my sight." He kicked it farther across the room, causing several of the pages to come out.

Abby felt crushed, rushing to pick up each one. It was God's word in print which soothed her and gave her strength. Wesley had torn her away from her home, her true love, and had ripped her scarf into pieces. Her Bible was all she had left.

Wesley turned back toward the chair and started to strip off. Abby's pulse quickened. Prayers ran through her mind and heart. God help me, please don't let this happen. Save me, let me be untouchable. Deliver me from this man's hand and his wicked plans.

Pulling off his boots first, he sat them beside the fireplace. Next, he removed his clothing, down to his long johns. He hung everything over the seat of the chair.

"This should dry them out in no time." Looking at Abby, he pointed toward his saddle. "Bring me another bottle of whiskey."

Abby wondered how many bottles he had. Doing as she was told she fetched the bottle. She stood as far away from him as possible and still be able to hand it to him. Grabbing it, uncorking it, he swigged several gulps down. Corking it back, wiping his lips with the back of his hand, he sat down on the floor beside the fire.

"Fetch that blanket." He pointed to the dirty one hanging over the window. With each instruction, Abby's heart grew more and more uneasy. No one was going to knock on the door to interrupt them this time, no one knew where they were. How was she going to get out of this? She wasn't.

She began to tremble, her hands barely worked as she took hold of the blanket to get it down. After several attempts of yanking, tugging and pulling, the blanket finally tore loose, falling to the floor creating a big cloud of dust.

Coughing, Abby picked it up. Feeling suddenly stiff, her feet didn't want to move. The closer she got to Wesley, the more danger she was in. She inched slowly toward him.

He stood, impatiently grabbing the blanket from her. He spread it out on the floor in front of the fireplace. Laying back down on the blanket, with a wicked grin, he whispered, "Take off your clothes."

Chapter 17

A light knock came from outside the jail door. Josh swiftly wiped his eyes with his shirt sleeve, not wanting anyone to see his tears. Slowly the door began to open, Randy popped his head inside. "Are you alright Sheriff? Do you mind if I come in?"

Pretending to be unphased by the morning's events, Josh replied in his usually friendly tone, "Yeah Randy, come on in."

"I don't know what happened earlier and I understand that you probably don't want to talk about it. I just want you to know that I'm here for you." Randy put his hands in his pockets and looked at the floor. Josh could tell he was uncomfortable but appreciated his friendship.

"There isn't anything anyone can do to help or change things. It's over. Abby is married and gone forever." Josh walked over to his desk and sat on the edge of it. "I guess I won't be living happily ever after, like I thought I would." Seeing the wedding certificate on his desk, he picked it up and held it out toward Randy.

"There is something you can do after all." Josh continued as the deputy took the paper from him. "You mentioned that you and your father were going to purchase supplies for the store and would be traveling by the county seat on your way. Would you mind dropping that off to be filed? I can't stand to look at it any longer." Turning from Randy, feeling embarrassed he turned his face away.

"Sure, I can do that." Randy agreed and took the paper into his hand. For several minutes both men remained quiet. Randy shifted his weight from one foot to the other, finally speaking.

"I better be going now, Father is waiting outside for me in the wagon. Are you sure you will be okay without me for a few days?" Randy asked sincerely.

Josh gave a simple nod. Randy placed his hand on the sheriff's shoulder. "Hang in there, it will get better." Folding the paper, he put it in his shirt pocket and left Josh alone with his thoughts.

Silence rang in Josh's ears, followed by memories that played out in his head like a picture show. Abby's face, every conversation, each day spent together, it all rushed back to him. How could he have been so fooled?

He thought they were in love, but she only loved money, which he didn't have much of. Why couldn't he have been born rich like her, maybe things would have turned out differently? His mind raced back and forth, from being broken hearted, to self-pity, and then to anger.

She had played him for a fool, traded him for the first rich man that came along. Wesley Roberts had only been in town a couple of days. She must have flung herself at him the second they met. Why else would a man propose in two days?

Josh felt disgusted. Was he courting and falling in love with a loose woman? Maybe that was taking things too far. Get ahold of yourself Josh, you know better than that. His mind was all over the place. Each time he began to calm down, Abby's face would pop up.

He remembered the first day she arrived in Cedar Creek. He pegged her for a spoiled rich girl, and he was right. Why had he let his guard down around her? Girl's like her don't change. How could he have let her pretty face and sweet voice get to him so fast? He was a fool, a lonely one.

Being the sheriff had caused him to spend a lot of time by himself. Most of the conversations he had were with either his deputy or a criminal. He was desperate for companionship. Too desperate. That would have to change. He needed something to occupy his spare time and his thoughts. Maybe he would play poker with the men in the barbershop on Thursday nights, or go hunting or fishing with a few of the guys.

It wasn't the kind of companionship Josh really wanted, but it was enough and would have to do. He promised himself to run the other way, if any woman so much as even looked in his direction ever again. Women were nothing but trouble. They only thought of themselves, talked too much, needed constant attention, and were distracting. He didn't have time for any of that.

The more he thought about being rejected, the angrier he became. She'd made a joke of him in front of the entire town. People were probably laughing right now, or far worse, pitying him. He didn't want their sympathy. How had he gotten himself in this mess? How would he face Cedar Creek residents ever again?

Abby's face drifted into sight. The soft sounds of her giggles when she was tickled, her smile when she was petting Max, how her eyes lit up each time she saw him, all melted his heart.

Josh couldn't help but smile when he remembered the way she skipped as she walked when she was excited. Most of all he loved her voice. It made him feel at peace when she sang in the pew next to him each Sunday morning at church.

Lord, why did this happen? I love her so much. Why did you let her marry another man? Wasn't I good enough for her? Wouldn't I have made her a good husband? Before he could stop himself, bitterness and jealousy reared up to poison his mind.

Wesley Roberts was everything Josh wasn't. A wealthy businessman with fancy words and expensive things. Josh recalled seeing his saddle. It had carvings of wild deer and birds in the leather, with matching saddle bags. His boots were dusty, but looked as if they had come out of one of those fancy catalogues.

Josh felt silly for thinking it, but he supposed Wesley was even better looking than him. He saw the way the women around town looked at the stranger, smiling as he walked by them.

Wesley seemingly had everything, including Abby. Josh stood up and walked to the window. It was pouring down rain. When had it started raining? He had been so deep in his own world of thought, he hadn't noticed the storm raging outside.

After a while Josh's heart filled with bitterness. Abby was a woman who would do whatever it took to gain social standing and wealth. A sheriff's wife wasn't on that list. His mind was made up. Abby was not the woman for him. He was not going to spend another second dwelling on her. Life would go on and he had work to do.

Without warning, the door burst open with a strong gust of wind, letting rain pour inside. Josh rushed to close the door, but before he got to it, Reverend Anthony Johnson appeared, soaking wet. He was dripping water all over the floor as he hurried inside.

Shutting the door quickly behind himself, he turned to face Josh. Reaching in his pocket, R.J. pulled out a folded paper, and a small piece of material.

"Tell me she's here with you?" R.J. looked around the room with a worried expression on his face. Josh had never seen him so nervous before. "Is Abby here? Please Lord, let her be safe."

Josh wasn't sure why the reverend was so upset, but it was too late to change things. "She's gone and she isn't coming back. What's got you all riled up R.J.? Abby is a grown woman, capable of making her own decisions. Unfortunately, I wasn't what or who she chose." Josh didn't like talking about it, the wound was still too fresh.

"Gone? She isn't here. I was praying that she wouldn't go through with it. Do you know where she went?"

"I told you she's gone. Why does it matter where?" Josh snapped back.

"Dear Lord, please help that poor girl." R.J. mumbled, barely loud enough for Josh to hear.

"You don't have to worry Reverend. She was married this morning to a man who is extremely well off. She won't lack anything for the rest of her life." Josh's voice changed as he added angrily, "She got what she wanted. Those type of women are all the same."

"Married, Oh Lord, what has she done? It's much worse than I imagined." He paused, looking down at the paper he held in his hand. "You don't know what you're talking about Sheriff, and you have to help her. Abby Gibbs is as fine of a woman as I have ever known. How long ago did she leave?

What did the man look like?" R. J.'s expression grew serious.

"Why all the questions? I'm telling you it doesn't matter. Miss Gibbs wasn't what we all thought she was. The nice Christian, loving teacher was all a sham. I hate to be the one to tell you this, but she deceived us all. Don't worry about her, that little snake can take care of herself."

R.J.'s face turned red. He marched straight up to Josh, standing only inches from the lawman, face to face. "Listen here young man, you don't know what you're talking about! Miss Gibbs is a saint. I will not let you talk about her in such a manner. Are you going to help me find her or not?"

"No!" Josh stated firmly. "I certainly will not. I know you don't like to think of people in a bad manner, being a preacher, but that woman is a money hungry, gold digger." Josh crossed his arms defiantly.

"Enough!" R.J. threw the piece of paper he held in his hand down on the desk, along with the fabric. Josh instantly saw that it was a piece of Abby's scarf.

Josh picked it up. "Is this part of Abby's scarf? Where did you get this?" He reached down and took the letter in his hand. He asked, "And what is this?"

"Before I tell you more, do you know the name of the man whom Abby left with?"

"Wesley Roberts? Why do you ask?" Josh watched R.J. close his eyes and saw a strange expression cross his face. At that moment, Josh knew something was very wrong, an uneasy feeling spread across him like a wind blowing a fire across a dry field. He didn't know why, but in his spirit, he thought his life was about to change forever.

"I was asked to not show you the letter. Miss Gibbs wrote it to me in confidence, but under the circumstances, I feel it imperative you read it. Abby's life may depend on it."

"Why would Abby write you a letter? You're not making any sense to me." Josh looked at the letter in hand and then at the piece of scarf with questioning eyes.

"When you read it things will become clear. Please Sheriff, we don't have any time to waste. Read the letter." Something in the Pastor's eyes told Josh the seriousness of the situation.

In his mind nothing was going to change his opinion of the new Mrs. Roberts. But at the same time, in his gut he knew this letter was a key to unlock a mystery that would open his eyes.

Did he want to know more? What if the letter contained information that would hurt him even deeper? He didn't know if he could take more heart ache. Not able to stand it, Josh opened the letter and began to read.

A range of emotions flooded Josh as he read. When he came to the part where Abby wanted to save his life and that she loved him, Josh had to swallow hard. He kept his head down as he folded the letter and placed it neatly on his desk.

"Sheriff, now you know that she sacrificed everything for you. I'm not sure how it went from running away to getting married, but I can promise you, she did it save your life. There is more and you're not going to like it."

"More?" Josh's head shot up, he felt deep remorse for the things he had said and thought about her. He remembered asking her at the ceremony if she was getting married out of love. Her reply had an entirely new meaning. How could he have tossed her aside so easily. Why had he let lies poison his mind? He didn't have time to think about that now, he had to find to her.

He hurried to grab his gun belt and put it on. Then he collected the rifle from the rack on the wall. Checking the ammo, he cocked the rifle. Calling for Max, he was ready to go. Abby loved him that's all he needed to know. She said her heart would only be held by one man.

Josh's adrenalin was surging, his pulse was racing. She loved him and was trying to save his life. He would stop at nothing to get her back safe.

"Sheriff, there's more." R.J. said. "You need to know this man, Wesley, knew Abby from a long time ago." He pointed toward the chair.

"You may want to sit down to hear the rest of this." He waited for the sheriff to take a seat, but when he didn't R.J. insisted.

"When Abby Mathews, that is the name she was born with, was twelve years old, her father took her into a bar called Robert's Saloon looking for a poker game. That night he was killed, making her an orphan. Wesley took her in to live at his saloon. At first, he only made her clean and cook." Josh didn't like where this might be headed.

"Soon Wesley became abusive, beating her with his hands and a whip. The man carries a whip everywhere he goes, in case you hadn't noticed. At only twelve years old Wesley Roberts forced a little girl to become a woman."

A great anger rose in Josh. He wanted to kill Wesley. "I had no idea. My poor sweet Abby. R.J., I pray God has mercy on my soul because I'm going to kill him."

With a stone-cold face Josh went to the corner of the room and pulled a rain slicker off of the peg on the wall, he put it on. Max was by his side, ready to follow his master.

"I know it's hard to stay calm, but you have to. Abby needs you to be rational. Slow down a minute and listen to the rest of the story." Josh listened as R.J. continued.

"After several years of living under constant torment, Abby was rescued by a man named Dakota Russell. He took her home to his step-father and mother's house, John and Grace Gibbs. She was then adopted by the Gibbs family and has been living there for the past five years. Wesley didn't know where she was until he tracked her to Cedar Creek."

Things made much more sense to Josh now. The trunk that Abby was so careful with that day in town was monogrammed G. G. Abby was protecting it out of love, not because she was materialistic.

He had accused her being a spoiled, rich girl with a pampered life. Yet, she'd had the opposite. Never once did she speak negative or not have a smile on her face. Josh was deeply ashamed. It pained him to have thought so badly of her.

"The scarf that she wears was given to her by a man who ran the local store next door. He tried to help her escape several times, but Wesley's hired men roughed him up and broke Abby's arm. After a few times, the neighbor realized it was best to leave her alone or Wesley might end up killing her."

"One day the owner decided to order her that scarf, out of the catalog, as a gift for always helping him out around the store. It was the first gift she'd ever received with no strings attached.

It has meant the world to Abby all these years. She left me a piece of it, I'm assuming as a keepsake, after Wesley tore it to pieces out of sheer meanness. I'm convinced that man is of the devil."

Abby was the opposite of what he thought and now she was in the hands of a monster. He remembered the black eye she had that morning. Wesley must have given that to her, Josh would give him a black eye if he could catch him.

"I have to get her back. I can't let that disgusting man hurt her again." Tying the bottom of his gun holster to his leg, as he headed for the door, he called for Max.

"She is married to him. What can you do to help her now? You don't have a legal reason to go after them or arrest him. You can't prove he hurts her and she won't tell you otherwise. Josh your hands are tied. Let me go look for her, I'm an ordinary man, Cedar Creek can't be without a lawman."

Josh held R.J.s gaze. "I'm going after them. I will be Wesley Roberts worst nightmare. Every corner he turns, every step he makes, I will be there, watching. Abby may be his wife, but I will see to it that he treats her right, or answer to me for it. Reaching for the badge pinned on his vest, pulling it off, he walked to R.J. and pinned it on the reverend's shirt.

"I now deputize you as acting sheriff of Cedar Creek until Randy gets back." Josh whistled for his dog, "Come on Max, let's go."

They headed for the door. "This ordinary man is going after the woman he loves."

Chapter 18

This was the dreaded moment that Abby had tried to block from her mind all day. She knew avoiding it wouldn't make it go away, but held on to a tiny shred of hope that God would intervene. Just looking at Wesley made her skin crawl, stomach churn, and spirit sink. Frantically her mind began racing.

Where was God? Didn't He see her situation? God are you listening? Get me out of here, don't let this happen. Maybe He was tired of hearing her constant cry for help. Since she hadn't let Him guide her in the first place, she would have to follow the path she'd chosen and suffer the consequences.

With a drunken slur, obviously growing impatient, Wesley yelled, "I said take off your clothes!" His jaw grew tight and his eyes narrowed. "If you don't, I'll rip them off." Abby could tell by his voice that he was losing his temper. She had heard that same tone many times. He was capable of the cruelest of things.

She remembered when Wesley found out she was carrying his baby. She was only a child herself of thirteen. Horrible memories of that night washed over her. The door to her room bursting open, Wesley rushing inside in a state of rage. Thirty minutes later she lay unconscious in a pool of blood, and no longer with child. If the cook hadn't found her and fetched the vet to sew her up, she wouldn't be alive now.

Death right now seemed better than her life. It sounded peaceful, painless, and much easier than facing the evil creature that sat in front of her.

Her hands began to tremble as she unbuttoned her dress, letting it slowly drop to the floor around her feet. Stepping out of it, she bent over to pull off her shoes and stockings. The only thing that remained was her slip. Desperately wanting to keep her undergarment on, she paused, not wanting to be striped of everything.

Wesley growled again, causing her to jump, "Get over here." With his hand he patted the spot on the dirty blanket beside him. She forced herself to take a slight step forward, then another and another. With each one her heart beat faster and faster causing her to feel faint. Part of her wished she would pass out. Then she wouldn't have to know the sickening things he would do to her.

All too soon, she stood at the edge of the blanket. Her knees felt locked, her body frozen. She struggled to make them bend. Before she was fully seated, Wesley grabbed her arm and yanked her down, causing her to fall on her back beside him. His hand instantly came around her waist and pulled her body against his.

The rank odor of whiskey assaulted her nostrils. She had always despised the smell of cigars and alcohol. Turning her head away, she tried to hold her breath. Wesley's hand began to roam over her flesh. Every inch of Abby's body stiffened. She wanted to curl up in a fetal position and hide.

She closed her eyes, this is it, Lord have mercy on me. Help me make it through what is about to happen, she prayed silently. She suddenly became aware that Wesley's hand had stopped moving. He was holding eerily still. Not daring to move or open her eyes, she listened. His breathing had evened out and sounded louder, almost like a soft snore.

Could it be possible? Did she dare hope, could he have passed out? Was this her miracle? Had God heard her cries and rescued her? Careful not to move her body, Abby slightly opened her eyes, just enough to peek out. Without any sudden movements, she slowly turned her head to face him. His eyes were shut and other than the slight rise and fall of his chest as he breathed, his body was motionless.

After several minutes, Abby felt sure that Wesley was indeed passed out cold. As carefully as she could, she slid herself out from under his arm and then completely away from the sleeping man. Her heart was leaping inside. She knew it was only one night, but all she had was now, tomorrow wasn't here and she wasn't going to think about it.

Abby knew when Wesley passed out, he would sleep soundly until the next morning. If she ever planned to escape, this would be her best chance. Where would she go? Back to Cedar Creek and to Josh? If anyone could help her it was Sheriff Cole. A smile spread across her face. Thoughts of Josh filled her heart with pure joy.

Looking back at the man on the floor, her smile quickly faded. She couldn't leave. Wesley Roberts owned her and there was no legal way out. She was trapped. Hanging her head in despair she knew there was nowhere to run.

The soft crackles from the fire drew her attention. Picking up her damp dress and stockings off the floor, she placed them on the chair beside Wesley's to dry. He had hung his gun belt on the back of the chair. For one brief second, she imagined pulling the gun out of its holster, cocking the trigger and aiming it at Wesley as he slept. No one would ever know, she would never again be tormented by him.

Turning away she prayed, Lord help me, what am I thinking. Shaking the evil thoughts away she grabbed her shoes and placed them near the fire, beside Wesley's, to dry. Seeing the two pairs of shoes sitting side by side pained her heart. Why couldn't they be Josh's and hers? Why couldn't she be Mrs. Joshua Cole?

She told herself to stop dreaming of things that could never happen, wishful thinking was a waste of time. She forced her attention to a place to sleep for the night. Looking around the room, her options where few. Wesley had the only covering, the dirty blanket, and she wasn't sleeping there.

Taking notice of the saddle which was also placed near the fire, an idea came to her. She could lean against it for the night. She didn't want to sleep flat on the floor where bugs or spiders could crawl on her. She shuddered thinking about it.

Curling up against the saddle, Abby began to feel tired. It had been a physically and emotionally exhausting day. She didn't dare give in to sleep, in case Wesley awoke. She needed to remain alert and prepared for the worst. The fire's crackling and popping sounds were soothing, causing her eyes to flutter open and closed. Abby didn't want to close her eyes.

Wesley could wake up angry. Or even worse, want to finish what he had started. She prayed that he would awaken with thoughts of California. His love for money would push him to hurry home. She would stay meek, silent, and out of his way. The less he noticed her, the better. Out of his sight, out of his mind, she prayed.

She didn't look forward to getting to California, but she had a plan. She had made up her mind that she was not going to work in the brothel. She thought once Wesley was so far from Cedar Creek that Josh would be safe, she could try to escape.

California was a large state with lots of big towns. She figured if she could find her way to one of them, she could live the rest of her life without Wesley and unashamed. She would get a job in a wash house, a café, or anywhere as long as it wasn't a brothel.

As she weighed her options, picturing herself living in a big city, a yawn escaped her lips, then soon another. She grew sleepier and sleepier. It was no use, she had to get some rest. She would need her strength and wit to face Wesley tomorrow. Giving in, Abby let her eyes close as sweet sleep overtook her.

***

Cold rain pelted Josh the moment he opened the door of the jail. Max quickly tucked his tail between his legs and lowered his head. Josh knew his dog didn't like getting wet, but would follow his master no matter what.

Since the stables burned down Josh had been keeping his horse tethered under a make shift stall behind the jail. Hurrying around back for his horse, he had no time to waste. He aimed to find Abby before nightfall.

Pulling his hat down on his head, he pushed forward, through the nasty weather. He couldn't help but wonder why today, of all days, it had to storm. All traces of the couple would be destroyed making tracking them nearly impossible. That was where Max came in. That dog never failed to find anyone yet.

He looked down at his faithful companion, "Don't fail me now ole Boy!" Max wagged his tail briefly, then tucked it right back between his legs. "I don't like being soaked to the bone either buddy, but Miss Abby needs us."

As if Max understood every word spoken, he shot off in a barking run. Josh scrambled to mount his horse and catch up with his dog. Max went in the direction Wesley and Abby had rode off early this morning. Josh worried how a scent could be picked up, it had been raining heavily for hours.

Lord guide us to Abby and keep her safe, Josh prayed. The big, furry animal looked back toward his master, as if understanding, dug his claws deep into the mud for traction, and ran faster.

Wesley and Abby had at least three or four hours head start. The ground was muddy, making it hard for Josh and Max to make as good of time as he had originally hoped.

"Lord lead us." Feeling worried, Josh prayed a simple and to the point prayer. He imagined all sorts of things that could happen to Abby if he didn't find her in time.

The rain, thankfully, had let up to a drizzle. This was the break that he had been waiting for. He was able to push his horse a little faster. It would be dark in another hour, time was running out. When the sun went down, they would have to stop.

His mind darted to what he was going to do when he caught up with them. He couldn't just waltz up to Wesley and take his wife and leave. He wished it was that easy. Josh realized he had no idea what he was going to do. All he knew was if Wesley laid a hand on Abby again, he would answer to him. If he had to, he would kidnap Abby, and take her somewhere safe.

If he had to live the rest of his life providing for a woman he could never marry, he would. It was his fault that she was in this horrible mess. He should have known she wouldn't marry for money. He should have never allowed her to marry that man.

What if Wesley put up a fight? He was no longer a sheriff and he couldn't just go in and demand Abby. He could end up on the other side of the law and be the one behind bars. He needed to think this over a little more. As he rolled various ideas around in his mind, they all ended the same. A physical altercation, with only one man walking away with Abby.

Who was he kidding, Wesley already had Abby. "Lord what am I to do? How do I handle this?" No answer came.

The rain had completely stopped. Josh was very thankful but wished the sun would pop out. He was cold and longed to feel the warmth of the sun. Josh knew that it was wishful thinking because it was so late in the day. If the sun showed itself, it would be to set.

Suddenly Josh was aware that Max had stopped a few feet back. He pulled on the reins of his horse. "Whoa, whoa boy."

Looking back, Josh called out, "Come on Max, let's go, what are you doing?" Max ignored the calls of his master holding his gaze at the hillside. Suddenly Max started to bark taking off in a run toward the trees.

"Get back here, this isn't the time to go chasing rabbits." As loud as Josh called for his dog, Max kept his focus on the timber as he raced toward it.

"I don't have time for a detour. Max get back here this instant," Josh demanded "Max, Max!" Josh watched as the big dog completely ignored him. He was off the trail and heading further away by the second.

"What's got into him." Feeling angry and not having a choice, Josh pulled on the reins of his horse. Frustrated, he headed after his runaway dog.

***

Something soft brushed against Abby's leg, slightly waking her from a deep sleep. She swiped her hand against the spot, as if to push whatever it was away. Her hand paused, then remained on her leg, as she began to fall back to sleep. Suddenly, something scurried across her hand. Abby's eyes flew open as she sprung to her feet just in time to see a big brown spider moving up her slip.

With a scream she jumped up, frantically slapping at her slip with her hands, trying to brush the spider off. She danced around the room flailing her arms in a panic, attempting to rid herself of the brown creepy crawler.

While shaking her hair and slapping at her slip, she failed to watch where she was going. Without noticing she tripped over Wesley's sleeping body, causing her to come crashing down on top of his chest and stomach with a thud.

Immediately Wesley woke with a cry of pain. His eyes shot wide open, focusing directly on the girl who lay on top of him. Abby saw the fury building in his eyes. She tried to crawl off of him, but wasn't fast enough. Grabbing her by the arm Wesley shoved her halfway across the room.

"What are you doing? Trying to kill me in my sleep?" Hopping up from the floor, he began screaming at her. "I'll teach you not to put your hands on me. You'll learn your place." In a flash he headed for the saddle bag, retrieving his whip.

In a full terror Abby pleaded, "I wasn't trying to kill you. I saw a spider and accidently fell on you trying to get away. I'm sorry, please Wesley, I'm sorry." Wesley acted as if he hadn't heard a word she said and stomped toward her.

"You're not as sorry as you're going to be when I get through with you. This is long overdue. You stole all my money, leaving me to suffer at the hands of my creditors. I lost everything because of you. I bet you thought that you could take me down. Well you didn't and never will. Now it's time for you to get a taste of what's been a long time coming."

"Please, it was accident. A spider was on me." Abby begged, trembling as she spoke.

Grabbing her by the hair, Wesley yanked her to her feet. "I'm going to enjoy this," he smiled as he spoke. Abby's heart raced. She wanted to scream, claw, and fight him off. But she knew he was too strong to defend herself against and her punishment would be much worse if she dared to try.

She felt more terrified by the moment, thinking of what her penance would be. He pulled her to the corner of the room, tore part of her slip off, exposing her shoulders and back. He ripped it into strips and used them to tie her wrists together with them.

He draped her bound wrists over a peg on the wall, causing Abby to be hung, standing up, by her arms. She had to stretch, almost tip toe, to keep her shoulders from feeling as though they were being pulled out of their sockets.

It was more than she could take, she tried not to, but broke out in uncontrollable sobs. Hysterically she pulled at the material around her wrist, but it only made things worse. With each tug the binding got tighter and her shoulders burned as if being torn off her.

She could hear Wesley's cold laughter behind her. "I'm going to peel the hide clean off of you. Then when I'm done, I'm going to fulfill my husbandly duty, and make you glad you're a woman."

Abby could hear the darkness in his voice. The man who haunted and tormented her in childhood was a monster and cruel beyond belief. But the man behind her now, was pure evil itself.

Lord where are you. God please take me now, I wish I was dead. More tears streamed down her face. She knew by his voice that he was going to kill her in a terribly painful way.

The crack of the whip vibrated in the air. Her pulse raced, she knew the next one would find her flesh. She pulled and struggled to free herself, feeling like a wolf caught in a trap, either chew off your own foot, or die.

"Struggle all you want. You're mine forever. I intend to teach you to never cross me again." She felt the burn of the leather as it slapped across her exposed back. She bit her bottom lip, willing herself not to cry out from pain. She wouldn't let him break her spirit. He may destroy her body, but he would never take her soul.

Wesley pulled his hand back using all of his strength to thrust the whip forward. He watched as it sank deep into his victims' bare shoulders. Abby cried out, as the whip pulled away a piece of flesh.

Sounding very pleased Wesley spoke, "Didn't I tell you? I had just enough time to tie a shard of glass to the tip of my whip before the wedding."

Abby knew this was the end of her short life. She reminded herself death was better anyway. She would only have to withstand the pain for a while, then never again. Closing her eyes, she said a silent prayer, her last. Lord grant me enough strength to endure to the end, I'm coming home.

***

Max was charging full speed ahead, so fast that Josh's horse could hardly keep up. He wasn't sure where the dog got so much strength after being on the trail for hours, wet and cold. As the timberline drew closer, Josh finally saw what his dog knew all along. A small cabin sitting at the edge of the woods. It had smoke coming out of the chimney telling Josh someone was inside.

Adrenalin rushed through him as he approached and spotted Wesley's horse tied to the porch. His instincts took over. Once at the cabin, he jumped off his horse, Max was already at the door. In seconds, Josh was by his dog's side.

As he reached for the door latch, he heard the snap of the whip and he heard Abby scream. In a flash, Josh remembered the day he accidently saw the marks on her back while she was in the washtub. They weren't birth marks, they were scars from the whip.

His heart plummeted. He grabbed the latch to open the door. He had to get inside and stop Wesley. As Josh readied to open the door a second crack of the whip sounded. Not wasting another moment, Josh kicked the door open, revealing Abby tied to the wall with Wesley behind her holding the whip.

Max charged inside growling with his teeth bared. Wesley grabbed his gun from its holster on the chair and in a flash had it aimed directly at Josh. Max raced across the room jumping feet first into Wesley's chest.

The big dog hit Wesley with such force that both man and dog fell backward several feet. As they fell, a gunshot rang out. They hit floor with a loud crash and blood began pooling heavily around them. Both man and dog lay unmoving with closed eyes.

Josh's heart sank when he saw blood around Max. As much as he wanted to go to his dog's side, he needed to make sure Abby was okay first. Keeping his gun aimed at Wesley, Josh hurried to her.

Wrapping his arm around her waist, he carefully lifted her up, making it easy for her to pull her tied hands from off the peg. Not taking his eyes off of the man on the floor, Josh used his free hand to untie Abby.

"Are you ok?" He spoke with a concerned voice.

Abby's voice sounded weak. "Yes, it's only a few minor flesh wounds. They will heal." Looking over his shoulder she saw Max's lifeless body and began to cry.

"Is Max…?" She didn't finish the sentence. Josh pulled her to his side and held her gently against him, but didn't speak.

"Josh, please go to Max, I'm fine," Abby urged.

"Have you ever shot a gun?" He asked her suddenly. Abby didn't hesitate to answer him.

"Yes, once."

"Take my gun, keep it aimed at Wesley, if he moves, shoot him!" Josh spoke sternly. He meant business. He wasn't sure that Wesley wasn't playing opossum. Abby took the gun in her hands and kept her eyes glued to Wesley while Josh went to his dog.

Josh took hold of Max's back leg and pulled him off and away from Wesley. That's when he saw the bullet hole in Wesley's chest, right through the heart. That's when Josh and Abby both knew he wasn't getting up. Wesley had shot himself in the fall, shot himself dead.

Unexpectedly, Abby squealed with delight and pointed toward Max. Josh looked back down at his dog. His big, brown eyes were looking right back at his owner and his tail began to wag.

Bending down, Josh hugged the stunned furry animal's neck. "Max you're okay!" The dog wagged his tail faster and began licking Josh's face.

Chapter 19

Six months later

Abby woke with a smile. Turning her head to see her husband, who lay asleep beside her. She still couldn't believe she was Mrs. Joshua Cole. She had to pinch herself to be sure she wasn't dreaming.

Abby chanted in her mind, over and over, Mrs. Cole, Abby Cole, Mrs. Joshua Cole. No matter how many ways she said it, each one made her heart quicken. She stared at her husband as he slept. Careful not wake him, she gently traced her finger across his cheek. Her stomach had butterflies. All she wanted to do was curl up next to him forever.

But she wanted to be the best wife she could be and it would be daylight soon. She wanted to make her man a hearty delicious breakfast. Slowly Abby crawled out of bed, so as not to wake Josh. She hurried to the kitchen to begin cooking.

Max was right behind her. He followed her each day at every meal. She would occasionally drop a crumb or two, or give Max a piece of food. She hummed a happy tune as she busied herself in the kitchen.

Happiness had finally over taken her. She glanced around her kitchen and couldn't help but think how long it took Josh to save for the down payment to buy her this house as a wedding gift. He had surprised her with the keys to the little white cottage on the edge of town on their honeymoon. Her life was complete. She had God, Josh and Max.

"Hello Mrs. Cole," a deep voice sounded behind her." Abby's face flushed red. Though they were man and wife, she felt a little bashful. In the past, she never believed a man could be kind, loving and strong all at the same time.

For the first time in her life she knew she would always have someone on her side to protect and love her. "Good morning Mr. Cole. Your breakfast is almost ready." As she finished the last word, Josh embraced her.

He pulled her into his arms and held her tight. He whispered in her ear, "I love you as far as the east is from the west."

Abby leaned her head back into his chest and smiled. She didn't know how God had taken her from the dungeon of despair and placed her in a heaven on earth, Josh's arms. She would spend the rest of her life thanking God for her husband, Joshua Cole.

***

The door of the Cedar Creek jail opened. Josh looked up from his desk to see a short, thin man in a gray suit walk in. The man had a round, odd-looking gray hat, black shiny shoes, and he carried a brown satchel.

Josh thought the stranger must be from a big city, someplace far from Cedar Creek. If men folk wore something like that around here, they would be laughed out of town.

"Good afternoon, may I help you?" Josh stood to greet the man.

"Are you the sheriff?" The stranger spoke with a nasal sounding voice that would get on your nerves if you had to listen to him talk for a long period of time.

"Yes, I'm Sheriff Cole. Can I help you with something?" Josh watched as the man approached his desk, digging through his satchel as he walked. Josh could hear papers being shuffled around.

"Ah, here it is," The man said as he pulled out a small piece of paper. "Sheriff, my name is Mr. Glen Carrington. I was the late Wesley Roberts' attorney. I have settled his estate by selling his properties along with various assets. I paid all debt that he had, closed his bank accounts and settled all his final affairs. I have in my possession a bank draft for deposit, to give to the widow Roberts. I wonder if you might help me locate her.

"Bank draft? I don't understand." Josh wasn't sure how this man knew about Abby being married to Wesley or how he found her. The sheriff's guard immediately went up. If this was a trick or some way of hurting Abby, he would not allow it.

"Let me explain. When you shipped Mr. Roberts personal belongings back to his home, there was a marriage certificate found in his coat pocket. So, I am looking for Abby Gibbs Roberts. She is the only heir to his estate, therefore after the liquidation of all his assets, she has a considerable inheritance owed to her, less my fees, of course." Mr. Carrington hastily spoke the last sentence.

"How much?" Josh couldn't help but be curious.

"I'm sorry sheriff, that is Mrs. Roberts business. Do you know where I can find her?"

"As a matter of fact, yes. She is due here any minute to bring my lunch." No sooner did he say the word lunch, then the door opened and Abby walked inside carrying a basket.

Seeing the two men were in a discussion she said, "I'm sorry Josh, I didn't know you were in the middle of a business meeting. I will leave the basket and be on my way."

She pecked Josh on the check with a kiss and turned to leave. He grabbed her arm to stop her. Mr. Carrington's eyebrows came up when he saw Mrs. Roberts kiss the sheriff but he didn't say a word.

Josh gently pulled Abby back to him. "Wait, this concerns you." Turning to face the attorney, "Mr. Carrington, may I introduce you to my wife. Mrs. Abby Cole. We were married last week. She was married to the late Wesley Roberts."

Mr. Carrington cleared his throat and looked at Abby. "Mrs. Roberts..."

Abby interrupted him immediately, "Please, it's Mrs. Cole."

"Mrs. ...," not finishing the last name he went on. "I am here to finalize the estate of the late Wesley Roberts. I have a bank draft for you."

He handed it to her, "Please sign here and our business will be complete."

Abby looked at Josh, he nodded his okay. Once the paper was signed, the attorney bid his goodbye and hurried away. Only after Mr. Carrington left did Abby look at the amount of the bank note. She gasped aloud.

"What's wrong?" Josh asked concerned. Abby didn't speak a word, she handed Josh the paper. When Josh saw the amount, his eyes grew wide.

"What are you going to do with three hundred thousand dollars Abby?" Josh asked. He knew the horrors that Abby had endured from Wesley and felt that she deserved ten times that amount. He would let her spend every dime how she saw fit.

Abby stood in deep thought and began to smile. "I remember talking to Reverend Johnson once. He mentioned that he and his wife always wanted to start an orphanage. They never had the funds." She looked at Josh with a sorrowful expression.

"I want to keep as many young girls as possible from having to go through what I did. The way Wesley earned this money was horrible and wrong. Maybe something good can come from it after all. I want to give it to the Johnson's. Would this be alright with you?"

Josh's chest swelled with pride as his wife spoke, what a big heart she had. She was given more money than all the people in Cedar Creek put together and all she wanted to do was give it away to help others.

Josh grabbed his wife, kissed her, and said "That is a grand idea Mrs. Cole. I sure do love you."

***

It had been almost three months since Josh and Abby moved into their little cottage on the edge of town. Each morning Josh would grab a cup of coffee and head to the front porch. He enjoyed starting his day with the sunrise.

Abby was in the kitchen cooking breakfast, humming away. Josh adored listening to her as she made happy tunes because he knew her heart was full of joy. If anyone deserved joy, it was Abby.

Taking a seat on the wooden porch bench, Josh looked at the world around him. A mist arose from the earth causing the land to look mysterious and exciting to him. He turned his attention to the mountains in the distance. The sun was peeking over them, lighting the world with vivid colors across the horizon.

Josh looked to his left, at Cedar Creek. It was a peaceful town, full of the best people in Josh's opinion. Looking down, Max was lying at his feet. Josh raised his head toward heaven and spoke.

"Lord, beautiful mountains are on my right. Cedar Creek and its wonderful people are to my left. Max is at my feet and my sweet Abby is humming inside while she cooks my breakfast. It can't get better than this." His heart was very content and full of joy.

Abby stepped outside, "Your breakfast is ready." Walking over to Josh, she sat on his lap and smiled. She took her husband's big hand and placed it on her stomach.

"Say hello to your daddy" She spoke in a whisper, looking at her tummy.

"What did you say?" Josh asked.

"I said, say hello to your daddy." Abby smiled widely, nodding her head up and down in a yes fashion.

Josh looked back up toward heaven. "I was wrong, it just got better than this!"

***

Jeremiah 29:11

"For I know the plans that I have for you' Declares the Lord, 'Plans to prosper you and not to harm you, plans to give you hope and a future."

The End

Made in the USA
Middletown, DE
04 June 2020